This signed, limited edition of

SATURATION POINT

is one of 3,000 copies

SOLARIS

PRAISE FOR ADRIAN TCHAIKOVSKY'S NOVELLAS

"After reading *Ironclads*, I think I can count Tchaikovsky as one of my favourite authors. Highly recommended."
The Curious SFF Reader* on *Ironclads

"Tchaikovsky shows us yet again how versatile are his writing and storytelling."
The Civilian Reader* on *Walking to Aldebaran

"Tchaikovsky focuses the taut story in such a way that every detail is relevant, building towards a climax that feels like a perfect pay-off."
SFX Magazine* on *Firewalkers

"This time-looped dramedy is as funny as it is thought-provoking."
Publishers Weekly* on *One Day All This Will Be Yours

"Tchaikovsky knocks it out the park...
A cunning take on both fantasy tropes and heroes' journeys. He sticks the landing, too, with a last paragraph that perfectly pays off what came before it."
Locus Magazine* on *Ogres

"Once again shows Tchaikovsky's gift for worldbuilding... An amazing story on so many levels."
The British Fantasy Society on
And Put Away Childish Things

SATURATION POINT

Also by Adrian Tchaikovsky
from Solaris Books

Terrible Worlds: Revolutions
Ironclads
Firewalkers
Ogres

Terrible Worlds: Destinations
Walking to Aldebaran
One Day All This Will be Yours
And Put Away Childish Things

After the War
Redemption's Blade

SATURATION POINT

POINT

ADRIAN TCHAIKOVSKY

SOLARIS

First published 2024 by Solaris
an imprint of Rebellion Publishing Ltd,
Riverside House, Osney Mead,
Oxford, OX2 0ES, UK

www.solarisbooks.com

ISBN: 978-1-83786-174-3

10 9 8 7 6 5 4 3 2 1

A CIP catalogue record for this book is available from
the British Library.

Designed & typeset by Rebellion Publishing
Cover art & illustration by Gemma Sheldrake

Printed in the UK

1.

THEY ASKED ME, "When was the last time you saw Doctor Fell?" and the memory hole I tripped into was ridiculous. After all this time. Twenty years. I mean, I've moved on. I should have moved on. I haven't.

You get an idea of what your life is going to be. Post-grad, impressionable age. And then it isn't how your life actually goes, but try telling your head that.

In my head I'm in the jungles of the Zone still. Doing what I studied for. Some part of me never left. Twenty years.

I wanted to tell them about the last day on site, after the money ran out and they pulled the plug on everything. Me and Doctor Fell in the last of the bubble tents with the evac transport a grumble on the edge of hearing. Looking her in the eyes. Sharing the guilt. How she just walked into the trees. That's my crystal-clear recollection of it, two decades later.

Just turned and walked into the trees. I dreamt it a dozen times since; my mind is absolutely sure it happened.

But I didn't say any of that, because I know it didn't go that way.

She was on the same VTOL out of there that I was. You *can't* just walk into the trees in the Zone. The trees will kill you. The Zone will. In my memory she's not even wearing her hazard suit. Memory is fallible. Dreams overwrite the reality, fond fantasies inform the dreams. I've precious little evidence we were ever there, except for a redacted gap in my resumé.

She never let me in. I don't mean into the Zone. I mean into the real stuff. My research was peanuts. They asked me what the Big Project was, that Doctor Fell spent most of her time on, but I couldn't tell them. "Ask her," I said, and they just looked at each other. "We'd love to," said Glasshower, and Doctor Blake added, very quietly, "We think she went back in."

Now *I'm* going back in.

Session 2

I'M ALREADY MAKING a mess of this, of course. If this is going to be of any use I need to start again. I'll delete the rest. Rambling recollections. No use to anyone.

My name is Jasmine Marks. My name is Doctor Jasmine Marks. I'm a biologist contracted to Zeisuritan. Or I *think* I still am. I...

...don't know what my status is, actually. I should check that.

*   *   *

Session 3

I'M WAITING FOR pickup now. I want to keep a journal, like before. My track record with these isn't good, but I've set some reminders. I'm going to keep at it. After all, for the first time in decades, there'll actually be something worth recording that isn't crop yield stat analysis.

I've already screwed up the start of this several times. I'll go back later and clean it all up. For now, I need to get this straight before I forget something important. I'm going back to the Zone.

They came to me when I was going over the Plot Nine Yield numbers. That's what Zeisuritan does with my education. One of a team of six, Building a Better Rice. Our most recent crop is doing well, actually. Shrugs off the new strains of *Pyricularia grisea* and has improved tolerance to high salt conditions. Not glamorous, but getting people fed. The top three patented brands of dry-cultivation rice feed around forty per cent of the world's population and that's the market we're aiming to break into. Really, it was looking encouraging. We were due a bonus. I gave that up, to be here, waiting in an echoing hangar for the plane to come take me south.

It'd better come. If this turns out to be a hoax and they just dump me home with nothing to show for my time but three days to catch up on, then I'll…

I'll…

It was right after I broke for lunch, by which I mean, took my tablet out of the part of my flat that's my bedroom-slash-workroom and boiled some noodles while I caught up on me-time… by which I mean all the messages from my family about all the things they needed. I had thirty minutes before I had to log back in to show my supervisor I was working, and most of that was trying to eat noodles while talking to my aunt. Her side of the family's in a Morrowzon company town, built around one of their big distribution complexes. Cousin Bobby has a job there, but apparently this week it didn't come with any actual hours, and so he wasn't getting paid. Could I transfer Value Vouchers over to them so that they could get food from the company store? It wasn't the money, you understand. They *had* money. Aunt Charla was very proud of that. Suitcases of dollars, they had.

"I don't understand," she says. Aunt Charla is one of those people who take pride in not knowing about anything that's changed in the world in the last thirty years. "They wouldn't take notes. They wouldn't take cards. I showed them my balance. I'm in credit."

"Auntie, don't show your balance to people. That's how you get robbed," I tell her, and I know I'm going to have to explain the whole Corporate Value system to her again and she won't listen.

"They said there was rationing," she says, like she never heard of such a thing before. So I tell her that, yes, there *is* rationing. Does she remember how they passed the bill, right after that big storm and all the crop failures and the economy going south and all that? Apparently Auntie Charla is completely blindsided by this, like there weren't protests and shootings and the National Guard. And that leaves us trying to work out how I can transfer some of my Zeisuritan vouchers over into the Morrowzon system so that Auntie Charla and my useless cousin Bobby and the rest of them can show that they're vicariously valuable enough to be allowed to buy some of what food there is. Which, needless to say, we don't get sorted, so I know that'll be my evening taken up. Except it's evening now and I'm not doing that. I asked Glasshower to get his people to sort that for me. And suddenly I'm the sort of person who can say that and people say, "Yes."

I'm losing the thread here. I'm nervous. I'm sorry.

I ignored the messages. Because you get a lot of messages on the Zeisuritan channel and most of them are junk. Internal admin junk and external advertising that inexplicably gets through all the filters. I just sat there and, you know, did my *job* for an hour because they send you all this stuff and expect you to read it all and reply to it, except they don't actually budget any time for you to do that, so you end up trawling through it all after hours. Except then my line manager opens a window on my tablet. A shock, to see a human face intruding into all my nice clean numbers, and I see the blue telltale that shows my own camera's come on. We stare at each other's naked faces awkwardly. It's horribly intimate and unexpected. "Jasmine," she says, "you have a meeting right now you should be at."

All the usual—sweats, plunging stomach. What have I forgotten? What did I get wrong? Am I fired? No good can come of an unexpected work meeting. Except, when she flags up the request for me, it's not even Zeisuritan. External request, party by the name of Glasshower.

I protest. Three words in, my line manager tells me to take it. Right now. On Zeisuritan's time.

It's not actually Glasshower. The window shows me a sharply-dressed nonbinary, very much the cutting edge of corporate chic right now. All about the *job* not the gender, you know? The filter mask helps. Just about all I can say about them is they've got nice nonspecific eyes. We go through some basic ID security to make sure I'm me, and then they tell my line manager she's surplus to requirements and cut her out of the call.

I have had no opportunity to check any ID of theirs. They are, they tell me, Mr Glasshower's personal assistant. I have no idea who the hell Mr Glasshower is. He, apparently, knows who *I* am. He wants to talk to me about the Zone.

It's been a long time since anybody wanted to talk about that.

They tell me Glasshower's cleared it with Zeisuritan. I get chapter and verse about how my esteemed employer's being compensated for my valuable time. A little screed of electronic handshakes and nods to say that I'm on secondment for the duration. Just an interview, I'm told.

By the fact I'm waiting for the plane right now you'll understand it wasn't just an interview. I mean, I'm used to people understating the amount of work involved in some project or other—they say an hour and it'll be a day, you know?—but this was a spectacular level of false advertising.

And, "Sure," I say, because what else? Breaks up the monotony of the day, right? Except right after, my spyhole system tells me there's someone at my door. At my actual apartment door. Even the mail and the take-out only gets as far as reception in my building, and it's not like I have anything to say to my neighbours, good home-deskers as they all are.

"You'll have to excuse me," I tell the immaculate face of Mr Glasshower's personal assistant. "I need to call building security. There's somebody at the door." The thought of the intrusion is making me sweat. Sweat more, anyway.

"I know," they tell me right back. "It's me."

"The fuck?" I say, and they neither flinch nor smile. And there they are in the camera on my door, standing in their neat little suit, out in the vomit-green of the corridor, in my actual building.

"I could leave you to make your own way to Mr Glasshower's office," they tell me, "but it would be easier if I just drove you to the airport."

I said a lot of things like, "Drive me?" and, "Airport?" but it boiled down to "Your boss wants to meet me *in person?* Is he nuts?" But they're already sending over all the stats—air filtering and decontamination certificates for Glasshower's offices, non-contagion checkmarks for all personnel. A clean corridor of guaranteed non-contact with any of the current wave of contagion variants. And of course, Zeisuritan will have handed over mine. Not like they need my permission.

I get a mask on and open the door. There they are, large as life, which is a little smaller than me, but still terrifying. A real live human being I never met before has cut through all the barriers that are supposed to exist between the great outdoors and my flat. I'm seeing them in the flesh. They're right there.

They look me up and down. "Maybe," they suggest, "you want to get dressed." And I remember that I'm shirt and jacket above the waist and cargo shorts below, because my line manager's camera doesn't see that far and because the AC in my building isn't worth shit.

Five minutes later, I'm dressed and in a climate-controlled car, coasting along half-empty roads to the airport. It's the first time I've met someone face to face or left my apartment in four months.

I sleep on the flight. It's a weird luxury. I get to sleep on company time that I'm actually being paid for. Makes a change from having to make sure I've touched a tablet screen every minute, so they don't tell me I'm slacking off. When I wake up, I'm practically being poured from the plane into another car, one medically-grade-filtered AC system to another and only a brief moment of heat in between. And it's a dry heat. That's not *real* heat. I know. When we get out of the car it's in a cool underground garage, and then the lift, and then the office. In media they still show these places with the glass walls and the real views, but these days Corporate money burrows deep—underground or into the centre of buildings where you can properly control the temperature and light and humidity. Turning our backs on nature. Except if *that* were true, they'd have no use for *me*. It's like I'm a shaman. A link to the past and the world beyond and the wilds, all in one. All three the same thing.

I *don't* pass that particular revelation on to Mr Glasshower. Though he might have appreciated it. He isn't what I've been expecting.

So he's an old white guy, and that much *is* as expected. He's slouched at one end of a glass table, shirt open and no tie. A lot of lines about his eyes and mouth. I stare, don't come any closer than the other end of that long table, watch his lips tug like a smile.

"They checked your bloods in the car," he points out, and they had. That little needle-jab built into the seat arm, just like any vehicle that carries multiple passengers. "And everyone in this building gets checked on entry. You can take your mask off."

There are always new variants. Or straight up new diseases. I don't de-mask.

He shrugs. "I leave it to your conscience." It's fascinating, getting to stare at someone's face. Seeing all that moving flesh on a real person, not an actor—or some actor's AReplica, more like. Except actors and their mo-cap proxies are all touched up to perfection, and Mr Glasshower—he's about to introduce himself, but it's him—is a man whose life experience is sketched in the lines about his mouth. All those smiles and frowns and pain and anger and satisfaction, written and overwritten until he's unreadable. His eyes twinkle. I reckon he hasn't slept in forty-eight hours, at least. Doctor Fell used to get like that.

Doctor Fell, concerning whom we're about to talk.

"At least sit a little closer. I don't want to have to shout."

Then you should have just popped up in a window on my tablet screen and spared me all the travelling, is my thought about that. Probably it shows in my face, but that's the other benefit of masks, isn't it? Mulishly, I move halfway down the table, which seems to be enough.

"Max," he says. "Maxwell Glasshower. Neosparan Threat Logistics." A buzz from the slate in my pocket that means his credentials have just turned up on it. I open my mouth to say *Doctor. Jasmine Marks, Zeisuritan Verdant Metrics* and he nods the words away. "The fact that you're here," he tells me, "means I know who you are." Watching my eyes for a reaction.

A thousand rejoinders bustle up inside me, about all this casual spookshow intimidation. *Yes, yes, and now you're going to tell me my mother's name and what I had for lunch, and…* Except he might. I haven't head of Neosparan—who can keep track, these days?—but 'Threat Logistics' sounds ominous, and I only hope I'm not part of the threat.

The personal assistant comes back in then—I hadn't noticed they'd gone out. They bring in someone new—a woman, short and stocky, a mop of coarse, dark hair. Plenty of eyeliner and, as she pulls her mask down, plenty of makeup too. Utterly humourless. All the lines about eyes and mouth have been smoothed away with cosmetics, but I reckon she hasn't smiled or laughed since the womb, honestly.

"Doctor Lis Blake, Doctor Jasmine Marks." Glasshower waves vaguely between us. The PA's absented themselves again. "Jasmine, Lis's our technical advisor on this project. Lis, Doctor Marks here is our expert."

The PA comes back in with coffee: either the real thing, from one of the handful of places where it still grows—hence worth more than my annual bonus—or just really good fakawa. The timing is fortuitous because, if they'd been ten seconds earlier, I'd have spat mine across that nice clean glass table.

"Expert?" I echo.

Blake looks at me as if I'm a fish that's gone off. "You were in the Zone," she says, like an accusation.

"Please." Glasshower rolls his eyes. "Let's not have any of that Strugatsky BS. The Hygrometric Dehabitation Region. No point mystifying this business any more than we have to. But yes, Doctor Marks. You were in the HDR."

"Twenty years ago," I say. "When I was a grad student."

Again that tired smile from him, and he says, "Well officially there's been no research presence since then, so we have to take what experts we can get. You were working under Elaine Fell. Why don't you tell us how that went?"

"I… can't," I point out, and my pocket buzzes, and that's all the waivers from my former employer releasing me from the labyrinth of confidentiality clauses that have shackled me for two decades.

Glasshower makes an inviting gesture and the pair of them settle back to listen. Which they do, for the next two hours as the coffee comes and goes. At some point I take my mask off, because I understand that I am Where the Money Is, and the AC will have the best filters and germ telltales, and I can actually sit there in the presence of two other human beings and not worry. And I worry, because you can't just banish habits that easily, but I dare anyway. And that little act of rebellion—like I'm with two cool kids smoking in a high school drama—paves the way for what's to follow.

For their part, they listen, and I know it's all being recorded. And surely most of what I have to say is in the records they've doubtless already cracked open and unredacted. They can get those waivers, they can *definitely* get hold of the formal write-up of Doctor Fell's work—both the stuff I was in on, and the stuff I'm not supposed to know about. Or maybe *that* isn't in the records, because they ask me about it. My own experiences, what else was happening around me, where Doctor Fell got to when she wasn't in my eyeline. And I stumble to silence, because suddenly the whole thing's like an inquisition, with me as star witness.

"It was a long time ago," I try.

"You still feel loyalty to her," Glasshower notes, with one of those sad smiles of his. "Speaks highly of your character, I assure you."

And I say they should ask her. I think I already said this part. I say that, and they say what they say: that Doctor Fell has gone back into the Zone, despite everything.

"Well, then, she's dead," I say, looking for a denial in their faces. Blake just stares back at me, as blank as if she's never heard the name of Elaine Fell before that second. Glasshower shrugs. "Well, that's the real trick, isn't it?" he suggests. "Getting word out of the HDR. Even knowing what she was doing in there. Nineteen of you came out. You are one of the few we've been able to speak to." For a moment I feel a deathly clutch, thinking myself a character in a cheap thriller whose peers are being systematically silenced to protect a secret. Then I understand: everyone else has a high-flying career that makes them too expensive, or engaged in more important or confidential work. I'm just the dregs of the talent, the only one sufficiently for hire. It isn't as though Zeisuritan can't fill my shoes while I'm here in this expensive office.

"Did you get on with Doctor Fell?" Blake asks.

"Well, obviously. She was principal investigator across all project sites. You had to—" Blather, blather.

"Did you get *on* with her?"

And I think of all the arguments. Her demands for data that she'd never explain, the way the flow of information went only one way. Me saying if I only knew *why* she wanted this or that, then I could be of more use. Her bulldozing over me, determined that I should just be a cog in her invisible machine. She infuriated everyone. She trusted no-one. She micromanaged one moment, left us to our own devices the next. I condense all this down for them, best I can. Probably the rest of it comes over in my pauses and my tone. If I have ever met a real-life genius in my life, then it was Elaine Fell. Maddening genius. Genius that had no time to explain itself to an adoring student. I straight-up refuse to tell them anything more than, 'She was obviously working on something big,' and I'd love to say it was out of fierce devotion to my long-ago mentor, but it's literally the extent of my knowledge. Something big, some in-Zone project that had been going on long before I ever turned up, wet behind the ears and fresh out of college—and somehow with a research placement in the most dangerous place on Earth.

But I tell them everything in my best wide-eyed student way, which is coming over a bit strong given I'm forty now. And Glasshower lounges and nods, and Doctor Blake blinks, infrequently. And not one of us says the obvious thing, because none of us wants to commit it to the recording. That is, if Doctor Fell has gone *back,* then the Big Thing she was doing never stopped being done out there. Somehow, even after the deaths and the end of the funding. Out in the Zone, where it kills you.

"If you were given access to your notes, and other documents from the HDR research projects, how fast could you get up to speed?" Blake asks me.

"Well I'd need time to—" I start, and then she helpfully clarifies, "In hours?" But that's okay, because it never left me. Because I have my own notes, absolutely prohibited under the terms of my contract, and I've gone over them more than once. The emergent ecosystems of the Zone, not just surviving but thriving in the wreck of what we did to the place.

I give them a small number. Neither of them bats an eyelid. They're used to people more naturally gifted than me, or else they know that, someplace in my head, I never left the Zone.

"Make a list," Glasshower tells me. "What you'll need to travel. I'll have someone buy it for you."

"Formalities," Blake coughs.

"Ah, yes." My pocket, again. Terms and conditions of employment, on secondment from Zeisuritan to Neosparan for 'the duration.' More daily remuneration, in dollars and Value Vouchers, than I'd see in a week. "The fuck?" I say. Not at my most professional, although I must have seen this coming.

"Formalities," from Blake, less cough, more actual word this time.

"Oh, right." Glasshower makes a dismissive gesture. "I mean, you're coming with us, right? Into the HDR."

I pride myself on my next moments because when he says that, everything in me freezes except for my mouth, which forms itself perfectly around the sounds, "Why are you going in?"

I get some images sent to my pocket. Satellite view of heavy canopy. A visible scar in the foliage. Broken trees, something bright at the end of it. Close by: a hint of wall—the aboveground section of one of the old field stations.

"Someone went down over the Zone?" I ask.

Glasshower rolls his eyes at the *Strugatsky BS,* as he called it. "Yes," says Blake.

"Then they're dead," I tell them.

"There's a suggestion of activity. We think they got underground." Again from Blake. Glasshower watching me intently. What was he looking for? I'm sitting here now, telling this, and asking myself the question. All that tired act was gone. He was like a hawk. Whatever it was, I don't think he saw it. Instead, he leans forwards, putting the laugh-lines neatly back into place. Probably it's supposed to be reassuring, but I haven't had a stranger that physically close to me for some time, so instinct has me scooting my chair back.

"Search and rescue in the most inhospitable environment currently known to man," he says, smiling. "But go we must. We'd very much like to have you along to warn us about what flowers not to pick and which spiders are venomous. And, if you like, you can even write up a monograph or something afterwards, redactis redandis."

"It's never too late to get ahead in academia," says Blake, po-faced. I'm still chewing over those last two words from Glasshower, and I just let them lodge in my head like undigested food. Only now, sitting here

Session 4

THE PLANE'S COMING in. Glasshower's PA brought me bags, all the things I asked for. New tablet—twice the tablet I could ever afford, and I wonder if they'll let me keep it. Change of clothes, toiletries, decent boots. Plus my measurements for a hazard suit—expanded a bit from my student days! There's Glasshower and the PA and me, but someone mentioned a team and a basecamp. I think we'll be coming down outside the Zone, first, to gear up. What's arriving isn't exactly a civilian tourist special, but it's nothing I'd go gadding about low over the Zone in either.

Session 5

REWIND BRIEFLY, DIDN'T finish the thought. Redactis redandis. 'After appropriate redactions.' A play on the phrase mutatis mutandis: 'With the necessary changes having been made.'
Which is a...
Which is a thing to say. When you're going to the Zone.
I realise I didn't say that I said, 'Yes'. But then I guess that's obvious. And I wonder, now, if Glasshower actually knew

Doctor Fell, either back then or later. He's a little younger than her, I'd say, but not so much. Because she had a bit of doggerel Latin she liked, too. I'd forgotten, but his little joke called it back to me. And if mutatis mutandis is a good catchphrase for the Zone, then so was her favourite.

Omnia mutantur, she said, *nos et mutamur in illis*. All things change and we change with them.

2.

Session 6

WE'RE IN THE air. No, that's confusing. I was in the hangar, wasn't I? Well, it's not that plane. I'm in a VTOL now. We're heading out over the Zone, packed in like fish in a tin. I'm knee-to-knee with Doctor Yang. Cheller's crammed in on my left and there's a big man whose name I can't remember on my right, bulky enough that his elbow's practically in my ear. He keeps looking at me as I'm saying this. Yes. Yes, you do. You can look away as much as you like, I saw you.

UNKNOWN: (*indistinct*)

MARKS: I am keeping a journal. We're going into the Zone. You don't think that's worthy of record?

CHELLER: You don't think they'll let you keep that, do you?

MARKS: We'll have to see, won't we? But this is part of how I work. It helps me order my thoughts. You never made study

notes for an exam, and then didn't have to look at them,
because making the notes fixed it in your head? It's like that.
CHELLER: You think there's going to be an exam?
UNKNOWN: (*laughter*)
MARKS: Will you just.

I am keeping a journal. I don't need your permission.

That's Cheller, by the way. Cheller is Mr Glasshower's
personal assistant, the one who came to my apartment. And
I'm not making a decent go of this, I realise. Let's catch up.

Session 7

OKAY, ORDERED MY thoughts. So we came down at what
turned out to be a mobile field station. Not like the hermetic
concrete bunkers dug deep into the ground that I remember,
but a little village of tents and prefabs thrown up and ready
to be taken down. Exiting the plane was like a hammer blow,
even though they'd been upping the temperature inside all
the way through the journey just to acclimatise us. Hot and
humid, instant sweat city, clothes sticking to you. Should have
kept my shorts on. Me, Mr Glasshower, Cheller—I'd got their
name by then. I was watching Glasshower because that kind
of corporate unflappability falls apart quick under pressure in
my experience, but the heat slides off him like a duck.

CHELLER: (*indistinct*)
MARKS: Like a. Like water off a duck. Right.

And it was nothing. It wasn't the *Zone*, yet. But it was close to. Cheller and I were gasping, fanning frantically, overheating. Glasshower just adjusted this white hat he had on, white with a black band. He was humming, even, deep in his throat. Gave me this snarky look like, *And I thought you'd done this before.* Then we got inside one of the prefabs and it had an AC unit, loud as a jet engine as it struggled to keep that thermoplastic box from turning into an oven. But the damp scrubbers were working at least, so it was a drier heat, and we'd all learn to value that soon enough.

There were over a dozen people already there and waiting, and Glasshower said they were our team. The moment I stepped in, my tablet received a group handshake with all their vaccination details, covered for every latest strain of each separate neovirus, certified safe. They looked…

Safe isn't the word I'd use.

Eminently professional, obviously. Corporate military, most of them. Fatigues and small arms. Made me wonder just who we were going in to search and rescue.

MARKS: (*faint*) What, you don't think it's odd? You can't
    shoot the Zone, you realise that, right?
UNKNOWN: (*indistinct*)
CHELLER: Crocodiles, right.
MARKS: Yeah, well, unless they've unionised or you're really
    wanting to exercise the Second Amendment, we won't
    need this many…
    Anyway…

So Glasshower introduces me as our native guide, which has them all boggling at me. There's one of the soldiers who's in charge, and Glasshower has him over. He's Crisis Parnallov, apparently, except I find out later he's Jakob Parnallov and nobody'll tell me where such an alarming nickname comes from. He looks me up and down and says, "You don't look like a *Marks*." And, okay, it's not the first time I get that, and my grandmother came off the boat with the name Mazarkian on her papers, but there was the Floridan Naturalisation Order, so we all got shiny new names fresh from Uncle Sam to save wear and tear on the western folks' tongues. And I give Crisis the stink eye because I'm here under Glasshower's umbrella and therefore not bullying material. We have a bit of an eyeball match right there, and then he decides I'm beneath his notice. His second's name was something like *Gorse*, I think, an even bigger man with some truly educational tattoos.

UNKNOWN: (*laughter*)
MARKS: Yeah, you know what I'm talking about.
UNKNOWN: You should see what he's got… down there.
MARKS: Jesus, no thanks.
UNKNOWN: (*laughter*)
MARKS: I mean I want to know how you know, now.
UNKNOWN: (*laughter*)

Anyway, I didn't get name, rank and serial number for the rest of the merc—*security* types. Glasshower had my elbow and was steering me over to a trio of civilians who were going to be my fellow advisors. Two of them were there just to look after the kit, and that reassured me a lot. Crisis's people had their own tech type, and here are two extra people solely concerned with making sure everything works. Which is good, because that's what'll keep us alive in the Zone. The hazard suits. And I remember things going wrong with the hazard suits.

I...

Jesus...

Session 8

I HADN'T THOUGHT...

We're over the Zone, now. No windows I can look out of, but I can tell. I swear I can. We're going into the Zone. *I'm* going back into the Zone. I've got to be crazy. I... They *died*. Karim and Toby died. On the last day. Two decades and whenever I thought about the Zone it was Doctor Fell and How Terrible We Had To Leave; the funding cuts, the loss to science. Not Karim and Toby. Finding them in their suits with the red lights still on. Telling everyone just what parts of their suits had failed. They must have called for help when things started to shut down. We didn't hear them. Nothing works properly in the Zone. Everything's always shorting out, burning up. Every day there was a struggle, not just to get our work done, but to *live*. Why am I going back to that? Why did Doctor Fell go back? What am I doing? I can't breathe. I...

*   *   *

Session 9

OKAY. WELL, CHELLER gave me a shot of something; thank you, Cheller. Feeling a lot better now. Everything fine. We're over the Zone. I can feel the VTOL starting to descend. I'd better get down what I need to.

My colleagues, then. Doctor Yang Jun—who's currently across from me and somehow managing to sleep despite the heat and the noise—is biosciences like me; biochemistry rather than ecology. I've actually read a couple of his papers on intermediary metabolism in accelerated adaptation, told him it was an honour. He's a little guy, few years younger than me but way more eminent. Good eyes. I mean, like me, he's kept his mask on all the time, so 'good eyes, good hair' is about all you can say about people, right? Of the two tech wranglers, Mayweather is way taller than me and has frankly incredible hair, really good hair. Yes, she does. Cheller agrees with me.

Mayweather is 'Investigations', whatever that means. I think mostly it means that the boring fix-it jobs go to Oskar, who's our other tech bod. Oskar's down the other end of the cabin, but I can hear him coughing. He's a thin, unwell-looking guy and he's got one of those phage-y coughs. The ones you never get shot of after you get something antibac-resistant and they have to shoot you up with a virus because it's the only way to fight the germs you've already got. And it's a shame, and it makes him a bit of a pariah, but I'm also glad I don't have to sit next to him. Anyway, Jun, Mayweather, Oskar and me, and then there's Glasshower—I am not ever calling that man Max like he says—and Cheller, and there's Crisis Parnallov and Gorse and their gun-having people. That's us. Done. And now we land.

Session 10

WE'RE STILL COMING in to land. I think we're doing circles while they look for somewhere we can get down. Because it's a jungle out there.

MARKS: (*fainter*) Hey, anyone here actually been to the Zone?
(*pause*)
MARKS: Don't look at me like that. It's a fair question.
CHELLER: (*indistinct*)
MARKS: Well maybe I am a bit buzzy from what you gave me, but it's a fair question. I mean, *anyone*? No? Just me?
GLASSHOWER: (*distantly*) Well, there's a reason we brought you along, Doctor Marks.
UNKNOWN: How bad can it be?
(*pause*)
MARKS: Jesus.

So anyway, I can hear the rain on the hull now. We're jockeying about, probably just above the trees. I don't think we're going to land. I mean, of *course* we're not going to land. There's no cleared space anymore, not even for a VTOL, unless we come down right on that crash-scar, and the foliage has probably begun to reclaim that already. They don't get how fast it all *grows* out here. I could show them. I actually have the data and the timelapse recordings now, back from when I was here with Doctor Fell. All in the data-dump Glasshower provided me with.

Oskar's getting up, about to do the air stewardess thing, only for a hazard suit. And obviously everyone here's had training already, surely. And obviously I remember.

I could put one on in the dark, even after all this time. I was in the Zone for four months, and almost every day in a suit. And the other days were when I didn't leave the field station. Because that's how it goes. I don't know if these people understand. I should be standing up like some prophet of doom, shouting, 'Take it seriously! It'll kill you!' but

Session 11

OSKAR'S DONE HIS bit. And honestly the new suits are sweeter than ours ever were. More fail-safes and a better interface. We'll be radio-linked and Oskar even came over to explain, if I wanted to keep a journal, how the suit would do that. All swish as you please, ease-of-use up the wazoo. Coughing sideways into his elbow as he said it, apologetic flinch every time. And I guess if someone with *his* lungs is trusting these suits to do their job, that should be as big a vote of confidence as you're going to get, right?

Karim and Toby died. It wasn't what finished us. The funding cuts were already common knowledge. I think that's why they pushed the boundaries like they did. They decided to go inwards. Karim said he wanted a look at the real business before we left. Doctor Fell's main project, not just our sideshow. The place she spent most of her time at. The other team. Talked Toby into it. Tried to talk me into it, too. I wouldn't bite. Had my final writeups to do, a few more tests to run while I still could, samples to secure. And it was going behind Doctor Fell's back. They called me *teacher's pet*.

We tracked their suits eventually. I thought Doctor Fell would round up a search party to haul them back the moment I told her what they'd done, but she seemed to take it in her stride. As if whatever was going on at the main site wasn't really as secret as all that. As if all the cloak and dagger of it had been just a game we'd been playing. Or else they'd already evacced and there was literally nothing there to see. So I went on with tying off loose ends and she went to make some calls. And later, still nothing from Karim and Toby, and I couldn't raise them on the radio, but that wouldn't be the first time we'd lost comms. And, eventually, the search party. And all that time they'd been lying there, first dying, then soon after that dead, and we'd never known.

I'm telling it now. And I'm trying to remember how it actually *was*. Not just how I remember remembering it. But memory is a hard disk that overwrites itself constantly. I can make it however I want, now. If I want the circumstances back then to seem suspicious, well, that's on me. I mean, if there *had* been something underhand going on, I'd have known, right? Something would have tipped me off. I wasn't as clueless as all that.

When Oskar was doing his talk about the suits, there was a lot of muttering and joking amongst the soldiers. They weren't taking him seriously. I should have said something. I know how it is, out there.

They're professionals. They know what they're doing.

But you can't fight the Zone.

And it occurs to me that they don't *get* the Zone. And that *nobody* gets the Zone. It's a part of the world now. It was established long before I came to skivvy for Doctor Fell, but back then it was novel. People were still talking about shrinking it, making it go away. Reclaiming the Dehabitation Region. Which I guess meant more people actually understood what it *was*. And since then, it's grown. I mean, that was why it was all tents and prefabs at base camp, right? Because we've accepted we can't undo the Zone. We can only hope that if we can get the overall heating situation under control, then maybe the Zone will stop spreading. And so the research camps out past the Zone's notional borders keep packing up and moving on. And we weren't in the Zone, in that prefab. Even though it was hot enough outside to boil an egg, and stepping through that air felt like having a warm shower in midsummer, that's not the Zone. It was just about at the mid-point of the curve that leads to it. The temperature-humidity curve. And listening to Oskar's spiel and the way everyone just grumbled through it, I understood that nobody quite understands what we're going into, not because it's new, but because it's old news. A jungle, crocodiles, hot, damp. The convenient markers that don't in any way encompass what the problem is.

I need to explain it to you. But we're landing now. They're

* * *

Session 12

I'M IN A suit. I'm saying these words from inside a suit. A hazard suit. One of the new ones, but it's just like it was. I can hear the hum of the cooling systems, which'll be more familiar than my own amplified breathing soon. There's a display showing me all sorts of metrics: heat, water, battery power, the name of whoever's speaking on the radio. Nice quality-of-life upgrades. We're not landing the VTOL. At all, I mean. They're just going to open up the belly and we'll go down on a rope. The vehicle's just about coping with the conditions outside, but Oskar says if it puts down and it sits around for any length of time he doesn't fancy our chances of getting it airborne again. We're going to be on our own until we call it back.

I've asked him about our communications and he went into rhapsodies, believe me. While we were playing meet and greet in the prefab, they had another plane fly over the Zone and drop a thousand little radio motes that sound smart enough to earn their own doctorates. They reach out and link to each other, he says, organise their own comms network, which'll be our radio breadcrumb trail to base camp, and thence to Doctor Blake back at Neosparan Towers. Doesn't matter how they fall, Oskar said, they'll work out an efficient coverage between them, and then they'll keep real quiet until he taps into the nearest one to send a signal, to stop anyone picking up on them. Only go live when in use, quick bursts of untraceable data. I asked him who exactly was supposed to be listening to us, and he just gave me a look like I don't know jack about these kinds of operations. In my day you had a single fixed landline

and even that cut out all the goddamn time. If we'd had this…
I keep thinking of Karim and Toby and their accident. If it
was.

Oh, God, I don't want to do this. Being in the suit brings it
all back. I've made a terrible mistake.

We're going. I

3.

THE MAN…

The man who sat beside me… His name was Yusuf Schreiber. He's dead.

He's dead. The man who was next to me in the VTOL. Who made jokes and helped me with the suit. He's dead. They're all dead, who were in the… eight of the soldiers, and Sergeant Gorse among them. Dead. They woke up dead. I want to say it was because they didn't take it seriously, because that would give it some meaning, some narrative. I mean, they *didn't* take it seriously, but it wasn't even that. It was just…

It could have been us, in the other… It could have been me.

I just…

It was over as soon as it began. They'll call the VTOL back now. I was here before. I remember Karim and Toby, and even

I didn't take it seriously enough. We should have checked. We should have… There must have been something we could have

Session 14

UNKNOWN: (*distant voices*)

Everyone's arguing. I'm not getting involved. My voice carries no weight anyway. I don't want to be Cassandra here. I'm… On the assumption that, if anyone ever listens to this, it'll be whoever goes into the Zone next, I'm telling you about why you don't fuck about in the Zone. I'm going to… lay it out for you. Or I could just say, 'look it up.' It's not magic. It's not even fucking high-level physics. It *isn't* 'Strugatsky BS' like Glasshower said.

UNKNOWN: (*distant shouting*)

Jesus. Right, no, it's just basic biology. It's simple, the way it kills you. It's just not what you're expecting. So I'm going to say what to expect, but… or you could just look it up and take from me that it's not an exaggeration and it kills you and you can't fight the Zone.

We dropped down on wires out of the VTOL. The suits had little belt things the wires went into. I couldn't work mine out. Yusuf helped me. I didn't know he was Yusuf, then. He was just The Soldier Who Sat Next To Me. Showed me where to clip in and how to hold on. We abseiled down like a crack commando squad. I felt very dynamic. I think we all did. I think that's why we messed up. Dropped down through the patchy bits in the canopy cover where the forest was still reclaiming the old field station. Gorse and some of the soldiers went first, with guns. I asked Yusuf what they were expecting to shoot.

"Jaguars," he said, and I don't know if he was being serious or not.

I told him you didn't get them around here, and that the Zone would kill them dead as us. But maybe there would be gators or some big snakes.

Then it was my turn to drop.

The hazard suit's fans were already humming calmly away, that vibration that becomes like part of your body soon enough, so that the lack of it keeps you awake at night after about a week inside the borders. The new suits were heavier than the old ones. They had light-drinkers like beetle wings on the backs, and piezoelectric harvesters and things to try and make them more energy efficient. I could have told them the back panels were a waste. It's gloomy down there under the canopy, like twilight all day and no moon at night. Solar gets you nowhere.

I checked the figures out as we dropped down the wires and into the world. Exterior temperature, 37° C. Relative humidity topping out the scale.

Thirty-seven degrees, which a little mental maths translated to just under a hundred Fahrenheit. I lived in Arizona for two years. Gets 15 degrees hotter most summers—Fahrenheit again. And, sure, you stay where the AC is, and you rehydrate plenty, but it's not like it strikes you dead like the hand of God if you go outside. Just slather on the serious sun-factor and wear a hat. Over the radio channel I heard one of the soldiers say just that, how they'd done a stint in Gabon, and *that* was heat. That was desert and it was dry bones and it killed you. This wasn't death, he said. It was life.

We were surrounded by life. That's what gets people. You tell them the equator and the heat and they think sand. They think just because a place isn't for *us* it can't be just about insane with *life*. It was the way that life was claiming and reclaiming the Zone areas that I was helping Doctor Fell research, back then. Because, when the process started happening, it wasn't what anyone expected. Around the time I was born, the best science brains in all the world were being confounded by it, just like the soldiers around me were.

And we helped it along. Because that was our job. Find a way to make the Zone profitable, farmable. I worked on a symbiotic algae that let regular trees photosynthesise using C4 pathways that can cope with crazy humidity. Adaptations stolen from aquatic plants that live surrounded by water twenty-four-seven because the air in the Zone is hardly less wet. Doc Fell had already introduced genes boosting positive xylem pressure, for when transpiration can't move nutrients up the tree because there's no evaporation happening even at canopy level. So some of what we're seeing right now is our work, twenty years on, but a lot of it is just nature.

There was jungle all around, when we dropped in. As far as the eye could see, which meant almost nothing because the jungle got in the way, and because the air was a haze of moisture. For the first minutes I kept trying to wipe away condensation on my visor except it wasn't, it was just the ambient air and the shade together making it look like we were underwater. And the jungle... You've seen video of the old rainforests, probably. It's not that, in the Zone. It's something more primordial. Different species rising to the challenge of the place and growing huge because the things that kept them small just can't compete. Ferns higher than your head. Rubber trees, kapok, palm, brazil nut. More cycads than you ever saw outside a dinosaur movie. Lots of huge waxy leaves running with water. And the flowers! The ultimate hothouse mix of orchids and phallic extrusions and goddamn gigantic rafflesia swarming with glittering flies.

A paleness through the fug of it turned out to be the field station. The concrete entryway was still there, but it had been cracked open by the operation of roots, pushed in by the growth of trunks. Two decades and the place was half-demolished, like an ancient Mayan temple.

The soldiers were spreading out in a ring, guns pointed outwards—at what? You can't shoot the ambient air conditions, and shooting the trees won't help. And everything else was... too much. Shoot the bugs, shoot the snakes, shoot the scurry of rodents and the skim of dragonflies. All the tiny living things around us. It freaked everyone out. I don't think anyone save me had been somewhere where there was just so much movement and activity going on. And if anything, the *livingness* of it all had redoubled since I was here.

I was just standing there in the middle, part of the cargo they were notionally protecting, bumping elbows with Oskar and Mayweather, Cheller and Glasshower and Jun. Us civilian types together. Except I could barely tell who was who. The hazard suits were all the same make, the bug-wing backs and the hard astronaut helmets with darkened visors, the built-in heavy boots and gauntlets and the silver reflective coating to bounce off all that sunlight we weren't getting. And they'd showed me how you could disengage the big gloves so you could get your hands out in just a fine mesh for delicate work, but I still didn't have the trick of it. And every one of us basically looking identical like a bunch of expendable NPCs in a virtua game. Glasshower and Cheller have bespoke suits painted slate blue, so I knew *them*. The rest of us are supposed to have names, I think, only that part of the prep didn't get done right. Oskar's has *Veidt* and Mayweather's has *Elhomey*, but most of the soldiers just have numbers, Jun's is blank and mine says *Emergency*, which everyone found very funny on the plane and no fucker is finding remotely funny now. And it didn't help that Parnallov, our head gun-haver, has *Crisis* on his, which makes the two of us look like we should be some crime-fighting superhero duo. Again, plenty of jokes as we landed. None any more.

Crisis Parnallov declared the landing site secured. From what? No idea. Oskar and some of the soldiers began setting up... stuff. There had been a bunch of packs dropped along with us, and I hoped nobody expected me to lug one about because they were about the same size I was, suit included. Two of them turned out to have tents in them—self-popping miracles of compact engineering that inflated out into a semi-rigid shell that shaped itself to the space we were in. Nice little bit of algorithmic design. By that, I divined we were sticking around the field station, at least at first.

They'd already gone into what was left of it. I got to see later. The interior—where the science had been done and people had lived, back then—was a wreck. There were roots like veins across every wall, cracking the concrete into crazy paving. There were things living down there. It was cooler, at least. Not actually *cool*, not comfortable, but cool *enough* that lots of critters had decided it made a good daytime refuge. Everything below two metres was flooded, and little runnels and channels trickled constantly down the walls. A whole ecosystem had sprung up there, from the moss and the bugs and the fungus and the lizards. I could have written a paper on it. My notes are on separate audio, but you can check up on how diligent I was being, even though it wasn't why we were here. In fact, I was down there far too long and missed the very obvious thing we *weren't* seeing. Feels really stupid, thinking back. I mean, it was right there—or rather it *wasn't*.

I remember just stopping dead—I'm with Mayweather and a couple of the soldiers at this point, poking about and finding that half the underground spaces had collapsed already, burying their secrets. After a little brain-straining I remember how to get a radio channel open and call for Cheller and ask them where the crash is.

They make an enquiring sound.

"The crash," I say. "The people we're searching and rescuing for. It was right on the field station, wasn't it?" Trying to remember that satellite view they showed me. And yes, easy to miss something a few metres off in this haze, but still…

Cheller doesn't have an answer—doesn't *answer*, period. I badger them about it and then I manage to get on to Glasshower himself—I'm still a bit startled that he's actually come with, to be honest. Assumed he'd be a stay-at-HQ sort of guy, but there he is. I ask him the same question, and there's a weird pause and then a slightly awkward laugh.

"Right," he says. "I'd forgotten we were running that rationale with you. There's no crash."

I point out that I saw the crash site and then, before he can say something to make me feel truly and utterly stupid, I catch up with: "Was that not real? You faked the image?"

"We did, yes," says Glasshower, unrepentant, still that little chuckle in his voice like it was a fun little prank. Like he assumed I'd seen through it instantly and was just too polite to call him on it.

I kind of splutter some questioning noises and he says, "Why? Honestly, we had two or three rationales ongoing, Doctor Marks. The rescue mission seemed the one that would play best with you. Cheller said we should just have gone with 'science expedition,' but that would be trying to fool you at your own game. You'd expect a whole raft of procedures that we weren't ever going to waste our time with, and you'd probably side-eye Crisis and his men too, when you met them. This seemed the easiest way to keep your questions to a minimum."

"Right," I say. "Well, then I have questions."

"They'll keep," he says, not unkindly. "For now, just this: we're investigating activity in the Zone. Someone's here and nobody's owning up to it. And so we're going on a bear hunt."

"No bears in the Zone," I say automatically. Because they'd die quicker than humans.

"Just hope that when we're done, you don't wish it was only bears," Glasshower tells me, and while there are suddenly lots of things going on that I don't like, what I hear in his voice I like least of all. Not meanness, not moustache-twirling evil, anything like that. He still has that world-weary humour thing going on. But I hear worry. Glasshower is The Man, he's In Control; he's not supposed to be worried about anything.

And I can go on strike. I can refuse to cooperate. I can demand to be taken home. And I'm not so naïve as to think that would go well for me. And the soldiers are all very pally and friendly right now, but that's because I'm on the right side of the us/them divide. And so I don't kick up a stink, don't make a scene, don't argue. I just accept it. Think about the money. Think about being back in the Zone.

Eventually Mayweather has done her checks and there's no sign anyone's been here doing anything since we packed up twenty years ago. I've been taking pictures with the hazard suit's camera, because maybe I *can* get some useful data out of this. Even in twenty years I can see major changes, ecosystem succession in action. Everything looks *more*—more commensal plant species—epiphytic orchids, hanging moss, strangling figs, aerial roots running down like power lines from the canopy above. And I think about Chernobyl. The nuclear site, the way it re-greened itself, radiation be damned. So quickly, too. All it took was no *us*. And obviously the Zone is tropical—I was about to say *equatorial* but some parts of it are past the tropics, even. It doesn't look like Chernobyl, but these are places humans retreated from fifty, seventy-five, even a hundred years ago. Not just humans, but our animal baggage, too. They used to ranch cattle right here, a century ago, but cows can't handle the Zone any more than we can. The speed that everything grew back and proliferated is truly stunning. Or not even *back,* because these aren't recreated ecosystems, but new mad-lib webs of co-dependence formed from all the species that found their way here. Everyone was talking about how climate change would kill the planet but leave people standing. And here we are, standing on a part of the planet that would kill us dead without our suits, and yet it's so full of life. Not even the post-human biome we always imagined—rats and ruins, dogs and cats, the human-adjacent fauna the spec-evo people said we'd bequeath the world to eventually. This is the return of the prehistoric wild, barely a mammal to be seen. That old joke phrase from last century's memes—*Nature is healing.* And I know, deeper in the Zone, there are towns, even cities, grown over and broken down just like this little field station. Places where thousands of people lived, where nobody can live at all.

By then it's late and the tents are up and we're camping for the night, ready to strike out in the morning. Strike out for where? Apparently Glasshower and Parnallov are on a private channel debating just that. The rest of us get inside the tents where climate control means we can take our suits off, empty out and sanitise the little slot-in/slot-out fanny pack that covers biological necessities, kick back and relax. We're all dead tired by then. Even in the suits, it's *hot,* you understand. Hot and claustrophobic and tiring to move around. Cheller and Mayweather and Jun are talking in quiet voices, but I just get my head down where they show me and go to sleep.

And when I wake up half of us are dead.

UNKNOWN: (*shouting, louder, cut off*)

Session 15

PARNALLOV: —all I'm getting are your fucking excuses!

VEIDT: I set up ours, Bakker set up theirs. Then Bakker checked my work and I checked his work. Just like the manual says. It was sound. There was nothing wrong!

PARNALLOV: Yeah? Well, it looks like *something* was fucking wrong!

VEIDT: The kit's defective. The pumps failed or the processor failed. The *alarms* certainly goddamn failed. Which means the whole thing's unsound. Which means how can we trust the other one?

ELHOMEY: When's the VTOL due?

(*two seconds pause*)

ELHOMEY: When's it due?

GLASSHOWER: There's no pickup. We press on.

VEIDT: Jesus fucking Christ.

ELHOMEY: With respect, Mr Glasshower—

GLASSHOWER: Oskar, I want you to go over the remaining tent, test every system. Be ready to move by noon.

*   *   *

Session 16

IT WAS THE other tent. It failed overnight. Failed and, in failing, killed everyone in it. Not immediately, but probably most of them died before waking, and the ones who awoke would have had... minutes. Stifling, prostrate minutes, already too weak to move, to call out. And if they'd called out, we'd not have heard, because the jungle is noisy and so the tents are soundproofed. And their radio was down along with the cooling and air systems. One of them, just one, was partway into a hazard suit.

Nobody here quite gets it. I just heard Amy Penser—she's one of the remaining soldiers, the woman—saying she's been hotter places. Saying she can see the reading on her HUD and it's hotter most days where her family are from. And she's right. Most of the States gets hotter days than this in midsummer. We're in the shade. You'd not even get much of a tan, under the trees.

So I'm going to set it out here. In case you, my unknown audience, are about to follow in our footsteps and repeat our mistakes. These are the words of Jasmine Marks, twice veteran of the Zone, survivor. Because it's not the heat that kills you, not alone. It's the moisture. Water, water everywhere.

One of the things we found in the Zone, back when I was working with Doctor Fell, is that the emergent ecologies that were recolonising the place were very light on mammals and birds. You got little ones, mostly nocturnal even where their ancestors had been diurnal. The big winners were amphibians, reptiles, bugs. Because hot and damp works for ectotherms.

We mammals think we're so smart, with our ability to regulate our own temperature, but that's not quite true. We *generate* heat, all the time. We're ace at cold climates. You never saw an arctic crocodile, right? We have a whole load of strategies for losing heat, too. Not a problem for little guys like mice, because their surface-to-volume ratio means they shed heat real fast. You get a big beefy mammal like a cow or a bear or an *us* and we have a lot more volume inside us relative to the area we can shed heat from. And that's not even taking things like clothes into account. And so we sweat. That's our big thing. We sweat out moisture, and it evaporates from us into the air. The shift from liquid water to aerial particles robs us of energy, and that's what cools you down. Wonders of science.

There's a thing called a wet-bulb temperature. Name comes from the weird-ass thermometer they used to use to measure it. It's the lowest temperature you can get to in a place through evaporation of water into the air. Past that point, sweat all you like, it won't shift enough heat to offset the amount your body is generating.

So back in Arizona or Gabon, say, you can still bring your personal thermometer down to where you can survive, because your body wrings you out like a sponge and losing that sweat to the air cools you down, because the wet-bulb is still low enough. But get that wet-bulb temp up to around ninety-five F or thirty-five C and your clever mammal body is pumping out more heat than you can shed, and you *cook*. The sweat does nothing. It's too hot, but the air is saturated with water. Everything you touch is running wet with it. You can sweat all you want, but there's no room for any more moisture in the air. In the Zone—what *defines* the Zone—is that: the temperature is really hot *and* there's so much humidity, that you're way past the wet-bulb temperature all the time.

Jesus.

So you cook. In the heat and the wet. You cook.

What *cooking* means is this. Being the thermoregulatory critters we are, we mammals are absolutely reliant on proteins that only work within a narrow band of temperatures. I'm looking at a lizard right now, blue and green guy size of my hand on the concrete of the field station wall, flashing his crest at me. He can get cold and he can get hot. He has a whole library of proteins for different temperatures, because his body temperature is a wild ride based on his environment. *We* haven't got that. We're biochemically really simple, we mammals. Efficient. Which is fine until we can't shed all the heat we make. At which point our proteins denature and all the various bits of us boil over and stop working. Even our fat reserves begin to liquify, like butter left next to the stove. Except *we're* the stove. We're pumping out that heat twenty-four-seven and it can't go anywhere. Which is what happened to Yusuf and Gorse and everyone else in the other tent. Which is what would happen to me if I took off the hazard suit right now, or if it stopped working like the tent did. I'd last half an hour max, and for most of that I'd be flat on the ground dying and knowing I was dying, but unable to do anything about it. Like everyone in the other tent.

I...

Have recorded this three times. My best teaching voice. Telling myself—telling *you*—why they died. To be in control of it. To give myself agency. I want it to help. I want *knowing* to help, or what's the point of me? I'm the expert, God help us all.

Session 17

THE OTHERS ARE arguing still. At least they're not shouting any more. That's probably the heat more than anything. Except for Oskar, who's working on the tent systems, checking everything's working because tonight we'll need it. The tent itself is collapsed down to a big but portable pack. Miracles of modern science. Didn't help.

I can't believe we're not just bugging out right now. I know big tough Crisis Parnallov wants to just call the VTOL; I heard all the choice things he had to say on the topic. Glasshower isn't having any of it, though. From the way Crisis is taking it, we might not get a positive response if anyone other than Glasshower actually puts in the call for evac, which is maybe why the boss hasn't been shot yet, because Parnallov sure as hell looks mad enough for it. Which will be awkward if anything happens to Glasshower. I mean, he's the oldest person here by about a decade, I reckon, and even in the suits it's going to be a strain to travel. Because apparently we're going to be travelling—going into the trees with whatever kit we can carry. For reasons. Reasons nobody is saying, and I have actually asked. And they ignored me, basically. The only usable intel I got—as Crisis and his people would doubtless say—was working out who actually *knows,* and who's equally in the dark. Glasshower and Crisis and probably Cheller know. Oskar and Jun don't. I can't say with Mayweather, and the two remaining soldiers—Amy Penser and Peter Lyle, for the record—were too impassive to tell, though I don't reckon they're in on it.

Session 18

MAYWEATHER'S JUST SUGGESTED we move at night, shelter out the day. I had to pull rank as the local Zone expert. Because you shed maybe a couple of degrees of heat at night, no more, and cooler air actually gets saturated quicker than hot. Unless you actually get underground, where it's cool enough to get under wet-bulb thresholds, all night gets you is it's just a lot darker— the miserable twilight turned into utter pitch darkness. These suits have good torches, but of course that's more drain on the batteries and we *really* need the batteries. Travelling at night will just be worse, basically. That's what I told everyone. We may as well try the tent tonight and move off in the morning.

Crisis is going to set up a watch rota. There'll always be someone awake and suited to make sure the tent stays working. And they can at least try and wake up everyone and get them into their own kit if things go wrong. That's the plan.

Then Mayweather asks if we could have slept underground, without the tent. And the answer to that's a 'maybe.' If we're travelling, then we won't just have a convenient ruined field station everywhere we go, and if we do find one it'll be half-flooded and filled with things that already consider it home and might be venomous. And it's a gamble that, even down there, conditions stay the right side of *habitable*, here in the Dehabitation Region. And so the tent remains the better option, as long as it doesn't fail.

Anyway, Glasshower's spoken, and by now the bickering is more over what we have to bring and what we leave behind tomorrow.

And one other thing. Glasshower to Oskar, something I probably wasn't supposed to overhear, only Oskar and I had been grousing to each other, and he left the channel open when the boss called him.

"When you've finished your checks," Glasshower tells him, "go over the other tent."

And Oskar, who's been working all morning on making sure we don't all die tonight, is pissed off with everyone but me and says, "I think we can safely assume that one *isn't* working," or something like that. And Glasshower says, "I want to know if someone tampered with it."

A bit of a pause from Oskar and then, "Sabotage?" in a strained voice. And Glasshower tells him to just do it.

And now I'm here, watching them all, faceless in their suits except for the blue of Glasshower and Cheller, and the names on the others: *Veidt, Elhomey, Crisis, 4* for Amy, *11* for Peter Lyle, blank for Jun and, though I'm not seeing it, *Emergency* for me. Watching them and thinking about what Glasshower said and how stupid it was to stoke that kind of paranoia in people, in a place like this.

Unless he's right.

4.

VEIDT: It was on my watch. It's my fault. Nothing like this
ever happened on my watch.

MARKS: (*indistinct*)

VEIDT: That doesn't change anything. This is my third tour
with Crisis. He's supposed to be able to rely on me.

MARKS: (*indistinct*)

VEIDT: Oh, no, me and Crisis go way back. So, yeah, he
shouts at me, I shout back. I just don't... This is my *job*,
right. Keeping this stuff running, I go all over the world
with teams like this. Cold weather, desert, high altitude. I
know all the kit.

MARKS: (*indistinct*)

VEIDT: Never the Zone, no. I mean who the fuck goes into
the Zone in their right mind, amiright? (*laughs*) But it's
not like the place is *haunted*. It's just physics. It's just

numbers. Nothing we can't beat with the right kit. I mean that's basically the motto of my whole *profession*.

MARKS: (*indistinct*)

VEIDT: I mean they told me 'search.' Not rescue, though. I guess that's not a cover story you give to people like Crisis. He's not the rescuing type. Enemy activity, they said. Which usually means some guys like us, only working for a different corporation. We thought it was just going to be a milk-run equipment test. I mean there's nothing here anybody even *wants*. Why would anyone...? No-one. There's no-one.

MARKS: (*indistinct*)

VEIDT: You caught that, did you? Boss-man wants someone to blame. Yeah, I looked at it. Didn't find anything. (*coughs*) No reason it failed. No cut wires, no sign anyone took a hammer to it real quiet like in the middle of the night. (*pause*) Although, I mean, all you'd have to do is just turn things off. That's the problem with places like this. It's like going into space. The baseline situation is that you're dead. You need everything working properly to climb out of that. It's like fighting gravity. You can stay up, but only because of the constant effort the kit's putting in to keep you there. You get me? Every natural rule of the place is trying to pull you back down to being dead. So if there *was* a saboteur, it's not like it'd be hard to pull off. But there isn't. (*coughs*) Goddamn. Because we're all in the same boat. Tent. Although...

MARKS: (*indistinct*)

VEIDT: Look, I don't want you to think I'm some kind of weird fetishist, but next time we're in the tent and out of these suits, you ever look at the boss-man's pits?

MARKS: (*indistinct, incredulous*)

VEIDT: I'm just saying. (*coughs*) Damnit. Time for the pills again.

Session 20

WE'RE ALL ON the pills now. It was Doctor Yang—Jun—who diagnosed the problem. The real issue is that we don't have the ability to treat the hazard suits properly—meaning full decontamination and separate storage every time we take them off. We were supposed to keep them in the airlock section of the tent, but after what happened nobody wanted any extra barriers between sleeping bags and suits in case our remaining tent died. And we've got Crisis's watch system, which relies on two people being awake and suited at all times in case of trouble. The fact that it's suddenly two people and not the original one suggests to me that Glasshower went bothering Crisis with his saboteur theory. So basically we're in one of those virtua games where you don't know if someone's a traitor or not. And I used to play the hell out of those back when I was a student, but it was never something I wanted for real life.

Anyway, what we've brought in from the outside are spores. They aren't actively malign, Jun says, but if you inhale them, they can mess with your pulmonary linings just by virtue of being big spiky particles you don't want in your lungs. Oskar's pre-existing condition meant he was the canary in the coal mine for it, but Amy started coughing soon after. The rest of us are okay so far. The real problem is the suit filters. Something about them says 'Please colonise me' to the spores, and so we're already seeing degradation in the circulation efficiency. Very small so far, but these things add up. Oskar's treating all the suits every morning with fungicides from our stores, but the spores are tough little fuckers, as he says, and he's having to ration the stuff. He's also checking in with base every morning, just in case our supply situation gets bad enough that we need evac. I, for one, am very glad he's doing that and that at least his clever node network business is working as intended.

It's safe to say that none of this is doing much for morale, which was already low for obvious reasons. I think Crisis is arguing with Glasshower on a private channel, saying we need to pull out and re-plan, but the old man obviously isn't having any of it.

I'm trying to get to know the others. Matters have gone from me being just baggage with a doctorate to being part of the team, because there's considerably less of the team now and everyone has to pull more weight. Literally. Apparently I can carry a pack after all, even if it's half the weight of Peter's or Crisis's. I'm also going to record the others—although after listening to my talk with Oskar, I obviously need to play with the suit's directional mic more. I haven't told anyone. We are very obviously engaged in secret business, to the extent that maybe only Glasshower knows what's what. I want to get a record of everything I can in case...

In case.

Everyone's very twitchy today. We maybe made nine miles yesterday, and partly that's me and Jun slowing everyone down, but mostly it's the *place*. Not just the trees, though the roots are chewing up the ground like you wouldn't believe. For half of today we were going through some village, and you could barely see anything that hadn't been torn to pieces by the trees and then painted over with moss and lichen. It just meant the actual going was really uneven, like climb up one mound of plant-buried rubble and stagger down the other side, over and over. And water, in every dip in the ground, and living things in every patch of water. Big snake went for Oskar, ended up with its fangs hanging off his boot, but didn't puncture, thank fuck.

I'm worn out. Everyone is.

Session 21

THERE'S SOMETHING OUT there.

There's some*one* out there.

It's not even my watch. I've been lying here, utterly exhausted. I can't get to sleep. I want to take something to push me over, but then I won't be able to stay awake later when it *is* my turn. And now Amy and Mayweather are spooked. They reckon something was moving outside, right by the tent. Amy's gone out with a gun and a nightvision filter. I've suited up. And it's ridiculous, because there's nobody. It's the Hygrometric Dehabitation Region and the D of that acronym means there's nobody.

Mayweather is talking to Amy now. They've included me in the channel. It's just Amy saying she can't see anyone, then moving, then saying it again. Once she said she'd found a footprint. She sent us a recording of it, but it was nothing. There's a lot of uneven ground, like I said. It was just a water-filled pothole. And if it *was* a footprint, it was one of ours from earlier. She said she could see bare toes there. I couldn't see it. Neither could Mayweather.

Mayweather says she saw someone today. Or thought she did. Didn't say anything at the time. Not there when she looked again. And visibility is so poor here, you start seeing human shapes everywhere in the mist. We're all very twitchy. I'm amazed nobody's been shot by accident yet.

Amy's coming back in, now. Mayweather's dousing her suit filters with more fungicide. The tent's sealed. It's my watch anyway. Me and Cheller, least useful members of the team. At least I'm already in my suit.

Session 22

PLAYED SOME GAMES with Cheller. I don't think the suit displays are meant for it, but Cheller is apparently very good at getting round software blocks. Which isn't a skill I'd advertise, frankly. Everyone must have got wind of the sabotage theory by now.

Anyway, they beat me enough for it to stop being fun. A moment ago, I was about to say I would do a round of the outside of the tent like Amy did, except I don't have a gun and I don't know how to make the night sight thing work, and it's dark as the inside of a cat out there. No light except the fireflies. When I was here last, there weren't fireflies, but I've seen a lot of species in the last few days that weren't here twenty years ago. The ecology of the Zone is a study in contradictions. It feels ancient—the voracious growth means there are layers over layers over layers, ecological succession so fast you can almost watch it happening. And the character of it all is… primeval, almost. Because mammals and birds were always only a garnish on everything else, and here that garnish is mostly gone. It's *hot*, and that means cold blood warms up fast and stays warm. I've been watching the lizards and the frogs and the bugs, and they're mad for it. It's like they're on speed and steroids all at the same time. And here's us and the rodents and the birds all still uselessly burning the midnight metabolic oil when there's a free energy buffet set out all the time, all you can eat. So you end up with something that looks like someone reconstructed one of those coal swamps from before the dinosaurs. And they say the dinosaurs were warm-blooded too, which means the Zone would kill them just as quickly. Too big, too hot. Dead as the dinosaurs.

Jesus, I'm rambling.

And the thing is, this isn't some ancient ecosystem re-asserting itself, because you can't cross the same river twice, with ecosystems. What we've got here is something completely novel, basically a huge number of invasive species thrown at a wall and we see what sticks. And the amazing thing is—the thing I published on, under Doctor Fell—is how complex it gets, how quickly. Like human presence is a pressure flattening everything out so all you get are the hardiest of survivors. Raccoons, rats and roaches, the three Rs. Here, all the elbow jostling has created a system of interactions, reliances, parasitism, symbiosis. I want to have ten years and an unlimited research budget. It's like a crucible. An environment with an excess of water and heat. If you can live here at all, then you really *live*.

I mean, there's a narrative of ecological change in the Anthropocene. You have some weird island or something with its unique fauna, and then we arrive, and soon enough the rats and the cats and the feral dogs, the pigs and sheep and cows have ground it all away, driven everything extinct and replaced them. Except here even the rats aren't doing well, because it's really good terrain for snakes and crocs and probably some sort of fuck-off enormous rat-eating spider I'm only glad I haven't run into.

CHELLER: There's a happy thought.
(*pause*)
CHELLER: You know you left this channel open, right?

Session 23

So I HAD a long talk with Jun when we stopped for lunch, only somehow I failed to record any of it, so there's that. He'd actually read some papers I co-authored—not the recent agric stuff, but back when I was here. Because, I suspect, there hasn't been much written since. Oh, there are half a dozen institutions maintaining some sort of presence outside the creeping boundaries of the Zone, but given the technical difficulties and personal discomfort involved in actually studying what's going on here, data is scarce. It's mostly satellite view and flyovers and there's a limit to what that can tell you. And there really *was* a crash four years back—as opposed to the fake one they cooked up to get me here—because even higher in the air where conditions are theoretically more tolerable, regular avionics systems are still under strain.

Jun's nice, in a quiet, withdrawn way. But I'm not entirely sure why he's here. He researches biochemical pathways, but from what he said, it sounds like it's in humans mostly. Which means he's the closest we have to an actual doctor right now, although I hope to God we're calling in the VTOL if anyone actually breaks a leg or comes down with appendicitis. He got cagey when I pressed him over precisely why he made the team. Instead, he wanted me to talk about my own work from two decades back. And, I'll be honest, he got me talking a lot, because it's been on my mind and it was good to share my thoughts with someone who had some insights to share. In the end I learned very little about him and somehow missed that he didn't really answer my questions directly.

Except the one thing I got was that, just like I'm on loan from Zeisuritan, he was on secondment from Mullern Opti SA. The space program guys, 'Making People Better,' 'Fit for the Future,' all that. And he must have seen my expression when it clicked, because he got a bit stuffy about it *not* being a eugenics program, just about helping people adapt to adverse environments. Which *could* sound like an explanation of why he's here, except it's not like he's suddenly going to pop up a surgical slab and get to work on us mid-mission. So what, exactly? 'Exactly' as in, that's *exactly* the question I somehow failed to pin him down on. Jun is a theory man, is my take. Which means he should be about as much use here in the field as a butter kettle. But here he is, at great expense and corporate wrangling.

They've got the tent up. Oskar's checking it over where it's splurged out between the trees here by the river. Or *a* river. There's water all over here, and it goes up and down like we're in an estuary. I've even heard Crisis and the others talking about tides. Except it's not. It's just... the Zone. So much heat that the air is sodden. You could wring it out like a rag.

And when it's too dark to see the river, I can check my suit display. Humidity's still as high as the gauge goes, higher than the daytime even, but though the temperature has crept down, it never dips much below a dalliance with the 95 Fahrenheit mark. We're still past the wet-bulb temperature, and nights in the Zone will still kill you. And all around us everything else bursts with riotous, enthusiastic life.

Crisis just sent the watch rotas over to our suit displays. I'm with him, past midnight. That'll be fun.

Session 24

MARKS: I don't suppose... I wondered... We haven't really got to know one another.

ELHOMEY: I mean, I normally don't put out until a third date, but I guess we might both be dead in the morning, so…

(*pause*)

ELHOMEY: Wow, okay, so that was intense. Sorry. Fuck. I wasn't actually coming on to you, by the way. That was just. Just… banter.

MARKS: (*simultaneously*) Badinage.

ELHOMEY: You win. Badinage. That is definitely a superior flavour of awkward conversational gambit. How are you holding up, Doctor Marks? Jasmine?

MARKS: Jasmine, please. And I can…?

ELHOMEY: Mayweather, then. Civilians got to stick together, right?

MARKS: I, er…

ELHOMEY: I am a civilian, yes. I'm not one of Crisis's little army men.

MARKS: Where did they drag you in from?

ELHOMEY: Portland, Oregon.

MARKS: I mean, I'm Zeisuritan, I used to—

ELHOMEY: Oh, I'm Neosparan. Glasshower's not just my boss, he's my *boss*. I'm Field Resources. And you're Emergent Ecosystems, or you were. And now you're Feeding Tomorrow, wasn't it?

MARKS: I think that was last year's catchphrase. It's hard to remember. What's Field Resources?

ELHOMEY: You ever see a spy film with all the little toys and things, periscope watches and laser goggles?

MARKS: Seriously?

ELHOMEY: I mean no, not either of those. But I test the
toys, basically. Or at least try to keep them in a usable
condition. I had three long range drones specially adapted
to high stress conditions that we abandoned back with the
other tent.

MARKS: Why?

ELHOMEY: Fuckers stopped working before I could even
get them into the air. Back to the drawing board. Heat
exchange died on its ass. Got a couple of little guys I can
deploy, though, but I've seen the size of the bugs around
here and I am not sure who'd win in a fight. So right now
I'm just double-checking Oskar's homework and—

MARKS: I mean, that makes me feel safer.

ELHOMEY: Did you hear that?

MARKS: What? What is it?

ELHOMEY: That was a shot.

Session 25

THEY'VE KILLED SOMEONE. Peter did. Saw something big moving
between the trees and trigger discipline lapsed. We were all
running over—me at the back, because I hadn't even registered
the sound. Crisis starting to chew Peter out over shooting at
shadows except then Amy got over there and found the body
and it wasn't shadows after all.

A person, right out here in the Zone. Not in a suit. Not in
much at all. A person. In the Zone. And a lot of shouting
and questions and, *How can this even?* And a lot of them

looking at me because I'm supposedly the expert and me just looking at the body after they dragged it over. Peter had shot him through the left chest: lung and maybe heart. I guess probably that would count as a good shot if he could have seen what he was aiming at, except given the mist and how all the fancy thermal imaging and whatnot they're supposed to have isn't worth shit here, I think it just counts as unlucky for his target.

The dead man was quite small and thin, and completely bald. In our lamps, his skin was a pale green. Not painted, not a trick of the light. A green man. His face was without any recognisable ethnic markers. Large eyes, small nose and narrow mouth. Not just bald, but hairless: no eyebrows, no eyelashes even. He was wearing a band of cloth about his... loins, I guess. An actual loincloth. It was... well, it was yellow and blue, quite faded, and I reacted to *that* enough that everyone stared at me a second time over. Because those were our colours, the colours our suits had been, back in the day. Doctor Fell's research team. Yellow and blue, to be easily seen against the jungle in case we fell over and someone had to come find us. Like we found Toby and Karim's bodies, by their yellow and blue. Except here it was so faded you'd not have picked it out at five paces. But *ours*, nonetheless. Salvage from one of the field stations. One of the deep ones I never went to, but which Doctor Fell did.

And he was alive, here. An inexplicable miracle, a Schrodinger's waveform collapsed by the barrel of Peter's gun.

Jun's prepping. Because Crisis and Glasshower put their heads together and then they came and told Jun and me that, while everyone else settles down in the tent, we get to do an open-air autopsy.

I point out we're not pathologists, except it turns out Jun has way more experience investigating dead bodies than your average biochemist, and that is a worrying thing to discover about someone whose maybe-eugenicist employer once had the motto 'Building People Better.'

So I point out that cause of death isn't exactly a Sherlockian mystery here, and Crisis prods my suit over the collarbone and tells me, "Every other fucking thing about this dead fucker is." Eloquent enough, I guess. I don't know what they expect us to discover, though.

Session 26

I DON'T KNOW what they expected us to discover. When Jun started cutting, I had to absent myself from the proceedings, and anyway all he found is someone who's mostly human. Big liver, apparently. Small kidneys and no loop of Henle at all, which means he wasn't designed with water retention in mind; go figure. Big spleen. Really very big gall bladder. Big enough that if we'd been anywhere else, and the patient hadn't already been dead, Jun would have had the guy in an emergency room getting it removed, except it didn't look inflamed, just real beefy. And you or me, we can have ours out and not really feel it much. It doesn't do a lot these days. John Doe here looks like he was getting serious use out of his. What kind of use? Jun had no answers, but he's taken tissue samples and he has his own little kit to run some tests and analyses.

What I saw, before I noped out of the whole business: Basically, one dead guy, bullet wound that was even nastier where it came out of his back. Except. I mean I've made my report. Written it down. And when they didn't believe me, I could go to the corpse and do the full stage magician reveal, show them how the trick's done. Extra eyelids, as promised. They go up; they go down. And look: for extra credit, who wants to shine a light into his dead eyes. Look, they glow like he's a monster from a bad horror movie. What that is, boys and girls, is a *tapetum lucidum*. Just like your kitty-cat back home. Dark-adapted eyes, perfect for the perpetual twilight.

Peter Lyle wanted to know if he shot an alien. Despite everything Jun and I said, I think they still half believe that. Too many fake alien autopsy videos where they lay out all the bits and say, look, this isn't just your everyday spleen, this is an *alien* spleen. These are *alien* lungs we've taken out of this lanky grey sucker with the big eyes. As if, in all the universe, there's only one way to do these things and only one order to stick the bits into a body. And then Oskar, who's thoroughly creeped out, starts talking about little men and prehistoric survivals and, well, elves and goblins, basically. Neanderthals and bigfoot and all that defensive 'well, you don't *know*' stuff. And, sure, John Doe is a cryptozoologist's dream, but I don't buy that any more than the alien theory. And I look at Jun and he looks at me, and I don't say it. I don't point out to everyone that his speciality is adapting humans to 'adverse conditions,' even if they're mostly talking long-duration spaceflight right now. Because here we are in some of the most adverse conditions in the world, and here's John Doe, who was just perfectly adapted to prancing about in them, save that inexplicably nobody built him to be bulletproof.

I think I'm in shock. I feel very calm and very numb, and I don't think that's within normal parameters right now. This is… huge. A living man in the Zone. Living until we shot him. Except. It's a man. A dead man. The miraculous thing about him was him not being dead and we took that away and now he's just a corpse. Unless Jun turns up the goods. Which leaves me with just two calm, numb thoughts.

Thought the first, in the wake of that: They knew. Glasshower—or Glasshower's boss—knew, hence getting Jun over. This is what Jun's our expert in. This very specific thing they didn't tell anybody was here.

Thought the second—and I'm not the only one to have this because Crisis has had Oskar set up lights and the watch will be outside the tent now, not inside it. Thought the second, then: we're being watched, and there's a whole extra suspect in the matter of the first tent.

5.

Session 27

WE'RE ALL VERY shaken, obviously. There was a real babble
of speculation once we were in the tent, but going nowhere.
Everyone looked at me as though I was supposed to have the first
clue. All I could say was that, when I was here last, there were
no weird bald people running around. No people, period. Only
us. And even then, suited and booted. And even *then*, some of
us died. So they got the story of Karim and Toby out of me, and
that only made everyone's faces longer, as you can imagine. And
Peter asks if maybe the green men killed them, and that's why
we never found out about them. Maybe there were always bald
green murderers hiding out in the Zone. His voice sounds shaky
and I guess he's trying to salve the fact he just shot someone, an
actual person, even though it was at least half by accident.

Oskar was saying about the tent, the one that failed, how
there wasn't any sign of vandalism. I mean, we have a dead

green guy in a salvaged loincloth. If someone had gone at the tent with an axe or a big rock, it's not like we wouldn't have noticed. And it's not like it's that easy to damage any delicate stuff that way, because the rubbery inflatable stuff these tents are made from is super-tough. If there's any question of sabotage—apparently this theory is public knowledge now, nobody acts surprised—then it was something sophisticated, not just locals going at it with sticks. Which means now we're all side-eying each other again, so good job Oskar.

The rota for tonight: Amy and Mayweather currently out there. Jun and Crisis next. Cheller and Peter. Then Amy again and me. Always someone with a gun, and the tent batteries getting a beating because of the floodlights Oskar set up, so he's already fretting about recharge rates and the lousy solar exposure you get under the canopy. Crisis told him not to worry about it. Glasshower doesn't stand watch, needless to say. Not that he's turned in yet. He was on the radio to Doctor Blake, earlier; now he's probably filing expense chits. Every so often he looks at me. It's that wry, dry, avuncular look, and of all of us he looks the most at ease here, the least spooked by what we've found. Not a man I'd want to play poker against. And then I remember what Oskar said. He's there in his white T-shirt, standard issue under-suit style with a Neosparan logo on the right breast. I remember stripping mine off because it was filthy with sweat—even in the suits, even with their top-of-the-range climate control, you get sweaty A-F. Except he isn't. Barely a stain about his pits or at his neckline. Did he change right into a new shirt and I didn't see? I don't think he changed. I don't think he sweats.

I don't think the green man sweated. Because we're in the Zone, and sweating is about as useful as a fire extinguisher in the sea. I want to talk to Jun, but he's working on his analyses with his little kit, and very obviously has zero per cent mental space to deal with anything else.

I have laid out my suit, ready to bolt into it. We all have. We all think the green men are going to come for us tonight. And why not? I've seen out there. We have these big lights on and all they do is illuminate a billion water droplets in the air, just turn the black to blank white, no actual improvement in visibility. And attract bugs. A million moths and beetles, some as big as your hand, constantly battering against the light panels, loud enough that it sounds like a hailstorm even through the tent's sound-dampening. Nobody's getting much sleep tonight.

Session 30

So WE'RE GOING home.

Or at least, Oskar's outside at the moment waiting for network connection to signal for the VTOL. It's coming for the body, I think, but it's coming for us, too. And I should be delighted about that, but I'm... weirdly ambivalent. It's like we just got to the very threshold of something and it's being snatched away. I mean obviously it's terrible here and I don't want to stay in the Zone a moment longer than I have to and people have died, but... I want to *know*. Working here with Doctor Fell was the most important contribution I ever made to the world, and now this. I wonder if Neosparan or whoever hired them will be building a research team. They'd have to consider me, wouldn't they? I mean I already know too much. I'm pre-overknowledged. Better to keep me close, right?

Glasshower made the announcement first thing. I'd been standing out with Amy for a couple of hours already. She was telling me about when she was on assignment near Lake Mead, when they were fighting over water access. She was saying all this was better, actually, because back then it was a lot of civilian action and militias and, just basically communities trying to divert the last of the water so they could cook and wash and, you know, drink, and the plants and factories deploying gun-havers like Amy under *Bottlespring v. Citizen Action.*

I remember the case, the precedent, how it was put over all very sanitized on the news. From what Amy said it was really, really nasty. Guerilla action and IEDs and children getting caught up in it. I kept wanting to start recording, but it wasn't really about the events, it was about her and what she'd done. Her trying to convince herself that even the Zone was better than that, because here nobody innocent got hurt. And I didn't point out about the dead green man we had wrapped in a tarp that had been crawling with inquisitive bugs all night, after the last of the damp-proofing gave and the lights popped so the insects didn't have anything to distract them from the scent of death.

Anyway, I was already wide awake when the coffee got passed round and Glasshower did his spiel, told us we'd pack up and evac today. And I wasn't the only one with objections, to my surprise. Mayweather said that we'd be at the main complex if we set out for it today, which surprised me—partly I hadn't thought we were that close to anything, partly I hadn't realised she was that well informed. Then Crisis weighed in, who'd gone hard for going home after the tent failed. Wanted to know why we'd even bothered with all this slog if we were just bugging out now? Glasshower said, basically, 'See that body out there? That's what we were looking for. That's what. So now we go.' Or words to that effect.

Cue more of everyone talking at once. Except me and Jun, who'd already worked out that they'd *known* the green men were out here—or *something* was out here. Glasshower sat down on the floor of the tent, just folding up, knees to his chin, gestures for us all to gather round like good children. It's story time. Hopefully a better story than the whole crash-search-and-rescue deal.

"You all signed the NDAs," he tells us, "so you know nothing goes any further. You're all frustrated. Nobody likes half a mystery. So there's a limit to what I'm going to say, folks, but I don't want that frustration boiling over into too many questions or loose lips, so let's see if I can bring you on-brand here." A self-deprecating smile at his own corporate BS. "A couple of decades back, there was a real research push around here. A lot of money thrown into keeping a bunch of scientists alive in prefab bunkers so they could study the place. Find out how to make use of it. Farm it, isn't that right, Doctor Marks?"

Singled out, I agreed. That was my field, certainly. I mean, the Zone is a growing area of vibrant biomass in the world. If we could find a way to actually make it work for us, it would make quite a dent in world hunger. That was the theory. Except making it economical turned out to be problematic—

the Zone degraded machinery and killed people. You couldn't automate, and you couldn't keep boots on the ground. We were making progress towards developing the crops, but I got told the people whose job it was to make it affordable drew a blank, and that's why our funding died a death.

"That was only the tip of the iceberg," Glasshower tells us. And it dates him, really; he's old enough to know what an iceberg is. "Agric is big business, certainly, but there was just as much work going into developing a workforce for the dehabitation regions."

People are looking at me again, but I obviously look way blank, and then he's calling out Jun.

"Doctor Yang?"

"I have seen some data," Jun says stiffly. He's younger than me, but he could still have been my opposite number, postgrad-of-all-work on *that* project.

"It was shut down," Glasshower tells us. "You will understand that I am talking about top secret, absolutely under-the-counter human experimentation, conducted without any state oversight, carried out by a corporation I am not even going to name, at sufficient arm's length that they had one hundred per cent deniability, and they *still* shut it down for ethical considerations." His grin is very sharp, inviting us to collaborate in rolling our eyes and saying *oh, what a world we live in!* "Except certain interested parties recently got wind that maybe it wasn't as shut down as all that. And you can imagine this came as a nasty shock to the people with the ethics who had expunged all mention of the damned business. And now we have our proof that they were right on the money.

And that's all we need. Time to pass it up the chain, folks. Not our problem any longer, thank you for your service, collect your paycheque on the way out."

Crisis looks furious. A man who wants closure. He doesn't say anything, but he has a whole tent of dead people on his ledger. Glasshower's act does not amuse him. Everyone else is stunned.

"Needless to say, they'll destroy you if you breathe a word of it," Glasshower says, still with that smile. "It's a mess, folks. It's going to get cleaned up. That's all. No further questions."

I try to talk to Jun, after that, but he's trying to get his analysis done still. For his own closure, I think. Something's got him seriously rattle—

GLASSHOWER: Doctor Marks, can you collect Doctor Yang
  and join me in the tent, please.
MARKS: I think he's—
GLASSHOWER: Now, please, Doctor Marks.

Session 31

GLASSHOWER: —should have an ETA for us on our air-
  evac, but until then, I thought we should have a little chat.
  Just the three of us.
MARKS: Four of us.
GLASSHOWER: Hmm? (*pause*) Oh, well, Cheller, I suppose.
  You count as a person, don't you, Cheller?
CHELLER: I've always thought so.

GLASSHOWER: (*chuckles*) You're too good at your job. You're like corporate furniture. Don't look like that, it means you're reliable. Now. Doctor Marks, tell me about your mentor.

MARKS: I—Sorry?

GLASSHOWER: Doctor Elaine Fell. When did you last have contact with her?

MARKS: I... It would have been right after they shut us down, she—

GLASSHOWER: No, seriously, Doctor Marks. We're done with the funny now. (*pause*) People have died, Doctor Marks.

MARKS: I am aware of that. Why do you—You think I'm hiding something from you? I'm not sure what—That I've had some sort of back-channel communication with Doctor Fell all this time? That I'm a fifth columnist? Wait—Jesus, you think the tent was *me*?

CHELLER: Well that escalated quickly.

GLASSHOWER: Actually, no. Not the tent. But Doctor Fell, yes.

MARKS: I... There's been nothing. Listen, I'd have talked to her like a shot. I even tried, after we were pulled out of the Zone. I thought she'd be moving on to something good. I didn't want to get stuck in... well, doing what I am actually stuck doing, actually. But she just vanished off the map, non-contactable. Meaning some corporation snatched her up for something off-grid, like we've all seen before. Meaning she... Well, never mind that. But she didn't contact me.

CHELLER: Meaning she probably had the chance to pick her own team and didn't pick you.

MARKS: Yeah. Thanks. Look, you can stare at me all you want. I know I'm probably a mess of little tics and tells and things they teach corporate management spooks to look for. I would absolutely have taken her call. But she never called, okay?

GLASSHOWER: (*chuckles*) I'm a corporate management spook, am I?

MARKS: Well, aren't you?

GLASSHOWER: I suppose I am. If that's even a thing.

MARKS: But you think this is her? Doctor Fell. You think she came back to the Zone and got on with... bioengineering little green men?

GLASSHOWER: Can we not call them that? Suffice to say we've also been trying to get hold of Elaine Fell ever since the HDR started throwing up error messages and we can't find her either. And you can believe that corporate management spooks like me have a lot more resources for finding people than you ever did, Doctor Marks. Doctor Yang, your conclusions.

YANG: Hm?

GLASSHOWER: I didn't ask you in here to keep minutes of the meeting. You've had more than enough time for a preliminary analysis.

YANG: I am rechecking my results. I want to send my data on your satlink for a second opinion, but we lack connection, apparently.

GLASSHOWER: Do we now? Well, how about you tell me about your *first* opinion.

YANG: I... There is evidence of proliferating paralogs for some proteins. My initial sequencing, and the tests I've run, suggest individual gene introns are under much heavier access.

CHELLER: Scientist says what?

GLASSHOWER: Cheller, please. (*clears throat*) But the point stands. What?

YANG: (*sighs*) Proteins are constructed from individual amino acids coded for by the active intron sections of genes. Because there are only a limited number of amino acids used in our biology, you can save genetic space by repeat-accessing the same intron for different purposes.

GLASSHOWER: And?

YANG: Paralogs, so they're like... You have a common protein ancestor and it mutates into multiple isoforms— All right, look: different proteins that are very similar but do slightly different things. Or work under different conditions. Again, more efficient to code for than building new from the ground up, because much of the structure is the same. A lot of paralogs. A lot of potential to manufacture protein variants. That's what I think I'm seeing, contrasted with the natural human genome. Or it's something else. Just a jumble of conscription errors. Redundancy and junk.

GLASSHOWER: Is there any way to know... generation?

YANG: You think it was *viable*.

MARKS: He.

GLASSHOWER: Is there?

YANG: Well, if we hadn't shot it, we could have asked it: take us home, meet the family.

MARKS: Him. (*pause*). Him. A human person that we killed.

(*indistinct sounds*)

GLASSHOWER: I know this is a tent, but would it hurt to knock?

VEIDT: I'm having difficulties acquiring the satellite.

GLASSHOWER: Right.

MARKS: Wait, is this… I mean, we've been fine so far. Is this because we…?

VEIDT: Jasmine, we've not been fine. Effective range of our transmitters is diddly over squat, with the atmospheric moisture and the canopy and the rain, and there's a stormfront coming on that's screwing us even more. It's been hell trying to check in every morning as it is. I need somewhere open to the sky at the very least. Mayweather says there's a clearing we can get to by noon.

GLASSHOWER: Fine. Let's pack the tent and make it happen.

Session 32

I DON'T KNOW what to think. We're in Mayweather's clearing— three downed trees, and a hole for the sky to come in. Actual natural light. That's not the problem. Oskar's set up some sort of wire antenna thing. Strung it up high. Trying to connect to one of the nodes out there. But listen. Listen.

I was just sat down on my own, about to start this entry, when I saw. I saw this was Session 32, and I thought, That's not right, is it? And I went back, and. And I'd skipped one. Back last night. There was just a gap in the recording queue. And obviously I assumed I'd screwed up, erased something, made a false start. I monkeyed around in the UI until I found the deleted cache. I thought I might have caught the talk I had with Amy when we were on watch. It wasn't. It wasn't that. It was...

Breathing. It was breathing, but not—I mean you get very used to your *own* breathing, living in a hazard suit. You tune it out, but it's always in your ears. This wasn't my breathing. It wasn't anything like my breathing. It was slow and shallow and I don't think I've ever heard anything breathing like that before. And there was a... an echo. Like an underground echo. Not like you get in the tent. Like someone had opened a channel to my suit radio, and just breathed in it weirdly, like some minimalist pervert. From somewhere else. And then deleted the recording, but they didn't tidy up the queue. I don't know what to think. I think I very much want the VTOL to come now.

Oskar keeps losing the network. The super-clever self-organising network. We should be in range of a node at all times, and they pass the call back until it reaches a transmitter in an area where the atmospheric conditions allow a decent satellite link. Hello, Operator, get me the sane world please? Except signal range is massively affected by atmospheric humidity, and to get any more humidity than this, we'd basically have to be at the bottom of the sea. And this morning he can't get a stable connection to the network. And we're all thinking it's the revenge of the green men, but he just says this is basically his life since we got into the Zone, and it's just that he wasn't saying anything because he didn't want to worry us. I mean what's one more worry, right?

UNKNOWN: (*shouting*)
MARKS: What? What's that?
LYLE: (*distant*) The fuck was that?
MAYWEATHER: (*distant*) Hold still.
LYLE: (*distant*) Fuck me!
MAYWEATHER: (*distant*) I said hold still!
LYLE: (*distant*) Fucking *arrow*?
(*shots*)

Session 33

IT'S ME AND Cheller. We're…

We're…

I mean, it was an *arrow*. Just sticking out of his suit. Sagging. Hadn't even gone in much. You see films, *Robin Hood*, they stick in, through the bad guy's armour, and then someone falls off the castle wall. This hadn't. The suits. They make the suits tough. Tear-proof. And Amy and Crisis were pointing guns into the mist, and Mayweather shouted at Oskar, who was half up a tree fucking about with his antenna and Peter was turning round and round trying to get the arrow out, but it was just too far for him to reach and I went forwards and told him to hold still and that's when the second one hit him in the back and I heard this sound, this whirring, this whining sound that went higher and higher, and then just as I thought it would start to hurt it stopped, and I didn't know, I didn't understand what it meant until he began staggering and clawing at the suit, and Oskar was shouting, he was shouting that—

The tent. Saying to get the tent up. But it takes time. He started to inflate it, but it's a good twenty minutes before it's pressurised and there's cool dry air inside and Peter's suit—they'd hit something. Something in the coolant system, the air system, the processor. Something. Because the suit's made to protect Peter, but there's a limit to what it can do to protect *itself*. There's so much tech in there and you forget, even *I* forget, how it's just that between us and the Zone. The Dehabitation Region, because you can't live there.

He would have been overheating almost instantly in there and—being inside the suit must have seemed worse than not being in it, even though it wasn't. He tore the helmet off, panicked, desperate. He was red as boiled lobster, gasping for air that was even hotter and muggier than he'd had inside the helmet. On his knees. I just...

I just...

Didn't...

Know what to do.

I watched him dying.

The shooting started then. Crisis and Amy hosing bullets into the trees. Splinter of wood. Whack of holes in leaves. Invisible damage. Lost in the mist. I saw another arrow hit Crisis's helmet and slant off it, leaving a scratch across the visor. He staggered, kept shooting. Then the next one hit Glasshower.

He'd just been standing there, very still, very calm. If he'd been fine, I think we'd have been fine. It smashed his visor, though. And the thing—I realised suddenly that the suits were tough, but they weren't magic. They were utilitarian survival gear, and all the cleverness of them was in resisting the hostile environment. Not primitive missile weapons. It smashed his visor, ended up hanging there caught in the fractured plastic that was left, the point before his face. And that was him, I guess. And who might have been next?

We were right out in the open, in that clearing where the trees had fallen. We didn't know where they were. Perhaps they were everywhere. We started running. Me, Oskar, Cheller. We civilians. Crisis was shouting something over the radio, but I couldn't tell if he was saying to go or not to go. Or just shouting. And we ran.

We didn't all run together. Mayweather and Oskar were both definitely moving, but I was following Cheller instead. We went into the jungle. I remember bouncing between trees, falling over, terrified I'd rip or break my suit. Breath roaring in my ears. Hearing radio from Crisis, from Amy, from Mayweather. And then not. And then nothing. Too much trees and distance and moisture to reach the other suits. And they were supposed to connect to the closest node of the network. I mean they'd pissed about a million dollars of kit out over the Zone, so we had plenty of nodes, right? Oskar said, *If you get separated, your suit radio will find the nearest node and it will connect you to the network. Just call in and sit tight.*

We're here in the jungle. Cheller says you always end up going downhill, if you just run around, and the river's somewhere close so probably they're right. We're sitting tight and we're calling in, but nothing. No nodes at all. Cheller says we need to walk in a spiral pattern out from where we are, until we make a connection. I don't even think I could do a spiral, not with the trees and the rough ground and the mist. I think we'd just do a circle, over and over.

The power indicator in my display says sixty-eight per cent.

Session 34

THE POWER INDICATOR in my display says fifty-four per cent. But at least we're four now. Four civvies together.

We walked along the river. Not actually on the bank, but keeping the sound of it to our right. Because it was the only landmark we were sure of. Cheller and me, intrepid explorers. We kept trying the radio, even though constantly trying to connect must have been an extra pounding on the suit batteries. And we had those solar panels, sure, but no actual sun, and one of Cheller's had got broken off somehow in the running around. And then we realised we were walking through a town, and that... made things worse, somehow. The terrain got worse—but it was when we realised that all those lumps and humps and overgrown hills were actually collapsed buildings that we just... stopped. Like we'd found a mass grave. And I'm sure it wasn't like that. Not like the Zone suddenly snapped into being and killed everyone. People who lived here moved away a century ago, ahead of the heat, the creeping boundary of the Zone. Which meant, Cheller said, they almost certainly died north of here when they finally reached some place where the locals *really* didn't want new neighbours. But I don't want to think about that. I mean, that's basically the backdrop to this half of the century, all over the world. The people who put up fences and the people who got moved on by the planet until they met a fence. Probably south of here there's the remains of fences put up by the people who lived *here*, before they had to move as well.

We're in the shadow of a tower block. A tenement. Probably wasn't too fancy even when they built it a century and a half ago. Half gone, now. Floors nine to whatever just turned into rubble that's all around us and painted over with roots and moss. The stump that's still standing, you can barely see an inch of concrete or rebar. The lower parts have been colonised by trees and everything higher turned into an unexpected windfall for plants desperate to claw their way out of the canopy's shadow and grab some rays. Every window socket is a riot of leaves and creepers, bright flowers, roots like gnarled hands. And I know everyone left, but in the back of my head, where I can't reach to clean it out, I'm seeing the interior full of a compost of bones everything's growing out of. And it's... like a riddle, isn't it? What's death and death, but life all over? And wasn't the planet supposed to die? Wasn't that the deal about human-generated climate change? That the world was supposed to predecease us? I mean, that certainly seemed to be what we'd agree to. That, okay, we'd destroy everything, but that was fine just so long as the last thing to get destroyed was *us*. And here's all this. Flourishing. Fucking *flourishing* in the death zone. Heat-adapted in a way we could never be.

Except we *can* be. I've seen it.

At least *they* haven't found us. But while Cheller and I were standing looking up at that building, I heard Oskar in my ear, and we called back—if Cheller hadn't been there, I'd have thought I was going mad—and Oskar zeroed in on us and they're here now. Him and Mayweather. And now he's gone four storeys up the tower with his goddamn antenna, and he's trying to raise the others or, if he has to, call the VTOL to get us out of here, and I so goddamn want to be out of here, and I…

Mayweather has an arrow. I don't know if it's one of the ones that hit Peter or Glasshower or anyone. She showed me it, and the association with death was so much that I didn't want to look at it, but then she forced me, waved it right in front of my face and I saw…

It had a black plastic head. It had plastic flights. It wasn't stone and bird feathers. She said it was printed. Where the hell are there working printers in the Zone? She thinks this is some weird spook show. Some corporation's here doing its work, trying to scare people off with fake green men. Except she didn't do the autopsy. That was no fairground animatronic or robot. Not that a robot would even keep *working* in these conditions.

VEIDT: (*distant shouting*)

ELHOMEY: What? Careful—!

VEIDT: (*rapidly approaching*) Got them! Crisis, anyway. He's coming here. The VTOL's coming here. We're meeting at the river.

CHELLER: Why?

VEIDT: Because the river's not *going* anywhere, and it's open enough for them to come down to us if I put up a flare. Now come on.

Session 35

UNKNOWN: Jasmine. I'm leaving this here for when you stop running. You probably think they're going to kill you like they did the others, but they won't. I've told them not to.

I am sending you a frequency, Jasmine. For the beacon. My beacon. Follow my signal. The creatures of the forest will let you pass. Because I say it.

You know me, Jasmine. I've watched your career. Such a promising mind, wasted in fighting the losing war between agriculture and climate. Trying to feed just a few more people for just a little bit longer. A noble but ultimately misplaced aim. I wanted to reach out to you before, Jasmine, but I couldn't risk people finding out where I was and what I was doing. But now you're here. They brought you to me.

When you check your records, when you've heard this, come and find me. Come and find my people. I'm sorry about the others, Jasmine, but they wouldn't have understood. You might. I remember you.

I'm waiting. I have such wonders to show you.

6.

WE'RE UNDERGROUND NOW. Cooler, a little. I followed the beacon. Doctor Fell's beacon. She is here. Glasshower was right. Until they killed him.

Cheller's still alive. Just alive. I keep giving them water. Their suit's gashed open. Their leg's all over blood. But we're far enough down. Far enough that it's cooler. Humidity still off the scale, but it was a positively chilly eighty-three degrees when I checked. Oh, and battery at thirty-seven per cent. I shut it down. I took off the helmet. I suffer with Cheller, because I need to save power for when I have to go out there again.

It's just us two once more. I can't believe... We had Oskar and Mayweather, Jun and Crisis and Amy. It was the whole gang back together. Now it's just us.

I have to say. What happened. Or nobody'll ever know.

We were at the river. Oskar had the VTOL coming, but he kept losing the network. He had a node of it, a physical thing, the size of your fist. I could see it spark in the saturated air when it was transmitting. But most of the time it linked to nothing. Oskar was raging, saying it wasn't possible. He'd just had a connection, clear as day. We were surrounded by nodes.

Crisis had reached us by then. He had Amy and Jun. They'd been playing with filters and things on the visors, trying to cut through the twilight murk, the constant hanging sheets of the fog. Amy was looking into the jungle—just an anonymous figure with that number *4* on her suit to say who she was. Gun in her hands, beaded with moisture. And Crisis, just a slightly bigger figure with that stupid nickname over his visor. Crisis decided Oskar's problem was due to enemy action. Someone had discovered our network and fucked it. Arguing with Oskar over encryption security. Oskar arguing right back that it wasn't possible. But you were wrong, Oskar. Even though you were the expert, I think you were wrong. I'm sorry.

Amy watching the trees. Oskar tinkering with the node, trying to troubleshoot and not understanding just how much trouble there was to shoot. Me, Cheller, Mayweather, Jun, sitting on the bank and waiting to be rescued like princesses. Jun had been with Crisis all this time. Had the sense to stick with the people who knew what they were doing. I was supposed to be that person. I was the native guide, the local expert who knew all the good bars and restaurants. I was useless. I was going to record another entry, then, but I felt too depressed, too much in shock. Peter and Glasshower were dead. Murdered, actually *murdered* by... by green men. The green men who couldn't be.

That's when I found her message. And her beacon.

I remember just playing it over and over. Looking at the others. Knowing I should tell them immediately what I had, and that every second I didn't meant I was a traitor. But knowing they'd think I was a traitor anyway the moment they heard it and so not wanting to tell them. Knowing that I didn't under any circumstances want to follow that beacon deeper into the woods. Knowing that I did. Part of me. The part that had known all along that my work at Zeisuritan was nothing but an exercise in pushing profit margins, and my real contribution to the world had been on hold ever since I left the Zone that first time.

I swear I was going to say. I had just decided I couldn't keep it to myself. I would bite the bullet, meaning telling Crisis first. He was very definitely in charge and he'd judge me the most harshly. I would get it over with, grasp the nettle. I *swear* I was about to.

Then Oskar screamed. I caught a bright flash, electric blue-white, in the corner of my eye. He was on his back, hands up, the suit gloves half-melted to him at the fingertips. The network had gone active mid-tinker and his node had suddenly started relaying someone's message. RF burns, they're called. I remember him joking about them, But that wasn't what did for us.

Amy started shooting. I don't honestly know if she saw something, or if the yell just spooked her. You could look into that mist and see an army between the trees. The mind tricks you. And so I don't know if I saw what I saw.

Strugatsky BS, Glasshower had said. The Zone. From that old book about a terrible place that you shouldn't go, except for the incredible, inexplicable secrets you could find there. But this wasn't Strugatsky, not then. It was full-on Ballard BS. The attack came from the river.

Jun had been looking out over the water. I remember his voice over the radio, sounding very calm: "What am I looking at?" I don't even know who paid him any attention except me, what with Oskar shouting and Amy shooting.

I looked round. The water was seething. I saw bodies push past each other in the black water. The occasional round eye staring out madly at us. Fish fleeing upstream in a slithering helter-skelter. In the dead hush the shots had brought, Jun and I just stared at the river trying to work out just… What? A scientific exercise based on insufficient data. Then I saw what was coming after them, and reached to pull him back, but I think I was pulling *me* back at the same time, because…

Alligators. The river was a coursing road of alligators, a tessellation of armoured backs and thrashing tails. Almost… carnival. Like it was National Alligator Parade Day. Driving everything in the river before them. Until they reached us. I was screaming at Jun, deafening myself, drowning out anything useful on our radio until Crisis muted me.

The first one just launched itself up the bank, a great belly-lunge with open jaws. Caught Jun by the leg and then he was gone into the thrashing water. I saw ragged streamers of his suit in the darkening water. Spinning reptile bodies. An orgy of gluttony. But they weren't done. They were clawing up out of the water, a tide of them, a tsunami of prehistoric flesh and teeth and cold little eyes. Crisis was shooting. Shouting at me to get out of the way.

Oskar still had his hands out in front of him. Cheller had been giving him a shot for the pain, and now they had him by the armpits, trying to haul him away. The only *away* was into the trees. I was scrabbling, slipping on muddy ground, clutching for roots. In my memory now, it's like a dream. Struggling forwards up the slope away from the water, but the world is dragging me backwards into that swelling flood of jaws and thrashing tails.

I saw the arrow hit Amy. It didn't even go in, just struck the solar panels on her back and bounced right out. She was on a slope, though, firing down at the alligators, and it knocked her forwards, took her off her feet with the sheer impact. She went in, headfirst into that maddened rush of reptiles, and they had her. Crisis was trying to get to her. She was screaming over the radio. I was running, then. I was with Cheller, hauling Oskar away. I don't know where Mayweather went. She wasn't with us.

When we were far enough from the river, we tried to call them. Crisis, Mayweather. There was nothing. We were the only three points in our own private network. Oskar said it was impossible. I could hear the tears in his voice. Cheller was.... Their suit was torn. A gator had made a go at them. They were trying to tie it off, seal it somehow above the knee. I did my best to help them. I didn't want to cut off the blood, but... I'm not a doctor. I'm ecology and agri sci. Their suit systems were still working, but they told me their display was all over errors because of the lost integrity.

I told them both about the beacon. I'd managed to unmute myself by then, after a lot of talking only to myself, which under any other circumstances would have been hilarious, but just then really wasn't. I talked very fast and didn't let them get a word in. I said, look, forget anything else but this. It'll be somewhere we can survive. Where Doctor Fell is. I felt weirdly detached, because they weren't saying anything anyway and I couldn't see their faces, so I couldn't know how betrayed they were. I just kept talking, trying to convince them until I realised they weren't trying to argue with me. Then, finally, I realised Oskar and Cheller had other things on their minds.

I looked up and saw *them*.

They were shrouded in mist, but very close. I could have taken two steps, reached out and prodded one in the eye. An eye with a doubled eyelid, like I'd seen in the autopsy. There were two of them that I could see. Probably more that I couldn't. One smaller than I was, the other about the same height but thinner. Lots of visible musculature, not much in the way of fat reserves, but then you wouldn't want the insulation. Bald as eggs. Staring eyes. *Click-click*, shutter-quick blinks that didn't actually interrupt their gaze. Standing there in the stifling, killing air as if it was nothing.

We were backing away. They moved lazily. An economy of motion beyond anything I ever saw. That sounds weird, but until I saw them, I never realised how fidgety and wasteful people are, all our twitches and tics and mannerisms. They stepped into our way, and then again. They were just *there*, where we went. Until I went the way of the beacon. Then they let us go. Just kept pace with us effortlessly. You barely saw them move, just looked up to find them standing somewhere else. One of them had a gun, Amy's or Crisis's. Strap slung nonchalantly over a shoulder, barrel pointing forwards and down.

The tiniest nod towards the path we'd been taking, as I locked eye-to-yellow-eye with them.

"Are you from Doctor Fell?" I asked them, but of course they weren't on our radio channel, and outside my suit my voice was barely audible.

"I am not going to be good for much longer," Cheller said. "If we're moving, then let's move."

We moved. I was so tangled up in the madness of what had happened and what was *still* happening that when the noise came I didn't notice it, thought it was just part of the chaos in my head. But it wasn't. It was the VTOL, come looking for us. A low drone that became a thunder of rotors, shockingly loud shockingly sudden. And Oskar broke for it. He had something, his maimed fingers fumbling it. Throwing it. I thought: *grenade?* but it gouted purple smoke that ballooned outwards in streamers to be eaten up by the sopping air. A flare, only it wasn't going to be alerting anyone. We couldn't even see the VTOL. But I could hear Oskar hollering on the radio, trying to get through to it: "We're here! We're here!"

Something intruded into my peripheral vision, clipping past the visor's extreme edge. It was the barrel of the gun. The green man raised it to his shoulder, sighting along the barrel in the manner of someone entirely proficient with firearms. The rapid-fire recoil of the weapon obviously surprised him, though. The barrel ended up pointing straight up, the bullets punching a line of holes from the undergrowth to the sky. And, midway between, through Oskar.

His voice cut off suddenly in a shriek, then something went in his suit, so I couldn't hear him at all. He was moving still, when one of the green men went to stand over him, drawing a knife. I tried to stop it—I actually went for him—but the other green man was in the way, gun cradled in his arms, and I couldn't. I couldn't willingly make myself move closer. Instead I let myself be herded to Cheller, and then I let the two of us be herded away. Away after the beacon, as Cheller got weaker and weaker and leant on me more and more. Until we found here. As soon as I saw this place, I realised the green men were no longer with us, and I couldn't say when it was they'd melted away.

Like the field station I'd worked at, all those years ago, but bigger. Like it would have been now. Overgrown, ruined. I despaired. I thought it was a joke, that beacon. Because surely this had been Doctor Fell's main base back in the day, the place she kept skipping off to, deeper in the Zone. Except it had fallen, just like all the works of human hands had fallen here. Fallen to the voracious encroaching of a new life that cared nothing for us or our little ambitions.

But it hadn't caved in, inside, and there was a clear route underground. That was the important thing. Our priority right then. And we went down, and...

And we're here now. The two of us. Down two levels to where the water precipitates out in the cooler air and we can live without suits. Where I could release the pressure on Cheller's leg and hope they're not just going to go septic. They're sleeping now, with the aid of a ton of painkillers. I don't know how they made it this far.

I need to sleep. And the little Crisis in my head is telling me, *No, keep watch,* but what could I do even if I sat up all night? What could I do if they came? They have a gun. They have bows and knives. They belong here. We don't.

Session 37

CHELLER WAS GONE when I woke, but replied to my panicked hail. They had gone further into the complex. I couldn't believe it. They'd used the aid kit on their suit to patch up their leg, then shot themself full of a frankly unsafe amount of painkillers and gone exploring.

"Just a little way," they claimed. Except that included going down a flight of poured concrete stairs slippery with running water. Their face was a tight mask of sweat when they came back. "There are lights," they said. And then of course I had to go and have a look.

Not on the floor below us, which was pitch dark, which meant I had to burn suit battery on the torch. That floor was part-collapsed, the walls veiny with optimistic root growth, warty with fungus. The floor was cracked, a miniature wetland, slimy with leaf-mould and soil washed down here, seething with movement. A microcosm of tiny lives and deaths. Just as above has been colonised by a million opportunistic species that drifted in and found a vacuum to inhabit, so it is below.

The worst extinction the Earth ever faced was at the end of the Permian period, right before dinosaurs pitched up. And for millions of years it was basically hog heaven for a kind of lizard-pig-looking thing called Lystrosaurus. You find fossils everywhere. It had a global mastery of the planet that would only be equalled when humans and our domesticated animals came along two hundred and fifty million years later. A lot of people have been talking about the Anthropocene extinction being as bad or worse—that's the one we're currently in, where we're driving everything to death by ruining half the planet and aggressively using every inch of the other half. Except here I am in the Zone, which we can't use or live in, and... some small weird voice in me says, *It's going to be all right*. No monospecies desert of Lystrosaurus-analogues for five million years. Seeing all these different things that blew into the Zone like drifters in a Western and found they could work with what's here. Food webs and synergies and a constantly changing cast of characters, but the *ecology* itself survives. Like a creature made up of other creatures, the ultimate hive organism. It goes on without us.

End of digression. Sorry, sitting here with Cheller asleep again, it's hard to hold a train of thought.

I found another stairwell, just as Cheller said. A deeper level. That was how these things worked. There should also be conveniences like air conditioning, plus doors and airlocks for a hermetic seal to keep the heat and the water out, but the main thing was we dug down, in our field stations. Got low, got cool, which meant if something failed you wouldn't be dead like the soldiers in the tent.

There are lights down there. Electric lights. Dim ones, red ones. Not friendly lights. Not the sort of lights anyone would set up by choice, surely. But lights mean power, obviously. And

I didn't see any sundrinker panels up top, not that they'd have survived the jungle, or found much sun to drink.

I went back to Cheller—they were still awake, then. They said they'd seen conduits along the walls. I checked and they were right. Not all the roots were roots. I followed them as much as I could. They went up to the surface, but no panels, like I said. I found one that went *into* a tree. Into the dense mat of its roots, anyway. Up top with my helmet on and keeping a nervous eye on my stored power—seeing the flickering telltale that said my own sundrinkers were trying to recharge me and getting nowhere fast. We'd always repowered at the tent before. The tent we left behind, with everything and everyone else.

Cheller snickered at me when I came back. "You're pissed," they said. "You're a proper scientist at heart. You're pissed you're not going to solve the mystery."

So I decided to theorise at them. "I think it's biomass power of some sort."

"Isn't that heat from decomposition?" they asked and I put on my best lecturing voice and say that, yes, and in a jungle environment there's a lot of decomposition going on all the time. A lot of stuff generating heat. And, up there, just a lot of *heat* in general, compared to the cool below. A differential, maybe. Something that could be used. Not geothermal, but *biothermal* power, somehow. I'm out of my area and just shrug about the specifics. But someone's found a way to generate power down there. Someone. Doctor Fell.

"And the other mystery?" Cheller pressed. "Our killer friends with the vegan tan? You figure out how they're walking round not being dead? Your Doc Fell playing Doc Moreau with the gators?"

"Impossible," I said, really hoping it was. "Something much more illegal than that. Jun worked it out." Poor dead Jun. "Multiple protein isoforms is what he said." Cheller stared back at me; a company man's Nonbinary Friday, not a biochemist. "The humidity doesn't kill you. It means you can't shed heat properly. You generate heat all the time because you're endothermic, and that's what that means. The heat kills you. Okay? Heat kills you two ways. Extreme heat like a fire just boils the fluid in your cells and they rupture and nothing survives that. Fever heat, or the heat up there, kills you because your proteins only work in a narrow band of temperature—the temperature our bodies maintain through our warm-bloodedness. Ectothermic creatures—you'd say 'cold-blooded,' though it's more complex than that—can't do that. Their body temperature goes up and down with their environment. So they pack instructions for a whole load of alternate proteins that take over at particular bands. I mean it's more complicated than I'm making out. A lot of the life you see out there is fine in these conditions because it's smaller than us—more surface area to less volume. And 'cold-blooded' creatures still generate heat they have to shed. It's complicated, but—"

"Those gators were *not* smaller than us," they pointed out.

"So, fine, they don't generate constant body heat like we do, and they're semi-aquatic and water helps, too. Much better at shifting heat than air. But like I say, they've got the proteins to cope with a range of body temperatures and we haven't. Our single set denatures if we overheat and then we die because those proteins are basically what makes everything in us work. Plus a load of other nasty stuff that also kills you, but mostly that."

"So, these green men…" Cheller prompted.

"So, these green men," I agree. "Jun thought they were designed for multiple protein variants, like a lizard is. I think our green men are cold-blooded."

"I thought that was a bad thing." Their voice was fuzzy at the edges as the latest batch of drugs took hold.

"It sucks if you're in the arctic," I agreed. "But body heat is all about activity levels. We get a constant high. Ectotherms are slow when it's cold, can't compete, easy meat for endotherms like us. Except out there, right now… they get free energy subsidies, and we're still burning fuel all the time. And they'd still need to be careful. Just moving around generates heat, and they must have limits, but…"

Cheller had nodded off by then. They're still sleeping now.

I don't want to leave them, but…

The lights, below. However many buried floors this place has. Someone's down there. *She* is. Doctor Fell. And she hasn't come up to me or sent her green minions, her *creations*, to come get me.

I'm going to have to go down. And they'll have help down there for Cheller: medicine, something. That's why I'll go. I'll be right back. I'm sorry.

7.

I WENT DOWN. I left Cheller, yes. I thought I could find something to help. No, not the only reason, but it's true still. Who knows what was left behind? But I had to know. What was there. What had been done. You have to understand. This was *it*. The thing we all knew about but never got let into, back in the day. The real focus of Doctor Fell's work, that all of our agriculture work was just peripheral to. The thing Karim and Toby were looking for.

She came back. She's here now, somewhere. Somewhere down there. That was what I was certain of. And yes, now, I can think of other possibilities. She could have left that message for me from the comfort of a penthouse in uptown Manhattan, for all I know. But I didn't think of any of that. I just went, because I knew I would find her if I looked the right way.

Down those steps, almost falling—worn down by the constant flow of water following gravity, treacherous with moss and decay, uneven with roots. Almost broke my neck. That would have been a fine end to it all. And the lights. I didn't want to turn my torch off and rely just on that dull red light. Emergency lighting, I was thinking. Hard to get your head round what emergency it actually meant. The growth of the Zone, the cancelling of funding, the deaths of our team, the ruin of the planet? We're not short of emergencies.

On the next floor, the ceilings seemed lower, the concrete walls and floor rippled and uneven. Conduits and wires were stapled to them, not set inside. A rush job, but when they built this place, they must have been desperate to get set up underground where the heat was merely unbearable and not actually lethal. Even down there, in that relative cool, I was all over sweat and swigging water from my suit reservoir fit to empty it out, losing a battle against dehydration, there in the wettest place on Earth. Everything in that structure was makeshift and hasty. No wonder the upper sections are coming apart.

And the roots, still. Here and there the wall was just cracked open, eggshell-style, a root driving out of it like a serpent. And *actual* serpents, plenty of them. Not an impossible coordinated wave like with the gators, just snakes living snake lives. But between them and the roots and the cables you just didn't know what you were looking at. Stepping on.

Some of the lights were out, but I reckoned these weren't the last dregs of a twenty-year-old system left over from my day. Someone had kept this going.

I found a map. Yes, there's a map down there. Old map, badly flaked and eaten by bugs, but I could just about make out a series of numbered laboratory rooms on it, and the legend *You Are Here*. It was while I puzzled that out with my torch that she spoke to me.

Doctor Fell spoke to me. To my suit. Had to hoick my helmet up onto the back of my head so I could hear, even. Spoke to me. Called me by name. "Hello, Jasmine."

The sound of her voice was... I'm not going to lie, it shook me. Took me right back. To when I was young, and had a proper future in research, and was going to change the world.

I said something asinine like, "It's you."

She asked me why I came back. I felt a stab of betrayal. I actually say, "Because you called me," which is kind of stupid and kind of not even true. I came because I got seconded out of Zeisuritan for this job. She only called me after we'd been here for some days and several deaths. I don't think that counts. But on the other hand, I guess it says a lot about the residual relationship we had, after all that time. And then it all comes out, as I'm fumbling my way towards where the labs should be, according to that map. How it's all gone to nothing and mundanity for me. How I'm doing mindless number-juggling for the benefit of some Agricorp's shareholders and not changing the world in any real way. Not expanding the frontiers of human knowledge. Or at least only in ways directly related to dividends. I bitch, basically. There, in the horrible red light, surrounded by snakes and with the very fabric of the place like Jenga all around me, I let out all the complaints and the bitterness I've been hoarding for two decades. You don't need to hear it.

"You could have called," I told her. "I would have come. For this. You must have gone straight back into the Zone. You must never have left. How long were you even working here before I arrived? That John Doe we looked at"—I took it as read that she knew absolutely everything—"he wasn't some kid. He was born before I ever came to the Zone. Was he even the first generation? What are you even doing here, Doc? I mean, Cheller said—said Doctor Moreau stuff, and I know it's not animals to people, but still, they had a point. Talk to me, Doc."

I waited, listening to the echoes of my own voice. By then I'd found the labs, but if I'd been expecting to step into a bright chrome-and-plastic laboratory complex, I was disappointed. All over dust and broken glass, ankle-deep in water that was still running away to some deeper part of the complex. Except, at one end, a rook's nest of cabling and monitors. No actual server room or anything. Terminal only, all very jury-rigged. And there were more. Ruined rooms with bolted-on tech of a variety of vintages, everything heavily insulated, the screens covered by rubbery, smeary films. There were more conduits and cables on the walls, older and newer waves of work. And a breeze. A movement of air through the tunnels. The sound of fans from deeper within, in a low, murmurous buzz. Differentials of temperature making convection loops as an incidental part of whatever system of heat exchange was powering up the place. Biomass generators, except the biomass was alive rather than compost.

I saw green men. I think I did. In that light, down there, it was hard to know. And I've seen how still they can be. Saw them slipping round corners, ducking into shadows. Not stopping me, or even confronting me. Not now I was where they wanted. Where their creator wanted. Or else I didn't see them, but my eyes were so keyed up that I saw them anyway. More than once I leapt back from an imagined arrow or knife; amazing I didn't smash something vital in my suit. And nothing. Always it was nothing. And I know they were there, even so.

"Jasmine?" Doctor Fell's voice came to me.

"Call them off," I told her.

She made an infinitely amused noise.

"Why would you even?" I demanded. "Why make them?"

"Why did I do it, or why did someone fund the project in the first place?" she said. "Two different things." And when I begged, she laughed at me. Just like she always used to. "Well *I* didn't," she said at last. "*That* project was already well underway when I first came to the Zone. Hidden in all the budgetary overspends and the trees. But I became a part of it. And as for *Why?* When a conglomerate of future-minded corporations gives you a bottomless well of untraceable funds and a team of top scientists with no scruples at all, it becomes all very, *Because it's there*. Because I had the opportunity to bring something new into the world, Jasmine, and if not me, then somebody else would do it. With that much money and tech, it was certainly going to happen. And the hard work went on elsewhere and beforehand. Easier places. A long-term project from back when the Zone was just becoming established and forecasters were looking ahead. And, of course, there were already people in Doctor Yang's line of work looking at the mutability of the human genome, how we might make people fit for Low-G, High-G, thin atmospheres, low oxygen, all that God-playing. A lot of the tech was already in place. It's just when people were thinking about changing people to live on hostile planets, nobody thought that would include Earth."

Yes, I pointed out that Yang Jun was dead, and she said that was a shame. I had the impression he was the only one of our casualties she was particularly bothered by.

"So you did it because you could," I accused her, and her reply was just:

"It seemed a worthy goal. A better reason than our backers ever had."

And I wanted to know what that was, and she told me, "Seriously, Jasmine. You have a part of the world regular people can't go into unprotected without dying of heat prostration in twenty minutes, but which clever people like you were supposed to be finding ways to farm and work and make productive. What do *you* think some big corporations might have wanted with a subspecies of humans specifically engineered to live and work in those conditions?"

I told her it wouldn't be allowed, and she laughed at me again. I had forgotten how much that laugh stung.

"But it didn't work," I pointed out. "They pulled the funding. They pulled us out."

"Oh, obviously it didn't work," she agreed. "They cut the money and the strings, got cold feet, didn't like the results. All the subjects were destroyed and all evidence of them erased or hidden so deep in black ops archives that it won't see the light of day for a thousand years. Farming the Zone was uneconomic, and if you're not going to have your plantation, then you don't need the slaves, right? But, Jasmine, I'll let you into a secret." Here she made her voice a grotesque sort of stage whisper. "Some of us on the team were a bit invested by then. Some of us didn't want to herd our creations into the gas chambers and then burn the papers. So we skipped that step and said we'd done it. And it wasn't like anyone was coming into the Zone to check. Nobody comes here. You must have heard that."

"And then you came back," I said.

"We came back," she agreed and by then I'd gone down a level, to where water was still running, but so were the fans. I'd naively thought that would mean cool. We passed through a room where there were big AC-looking boxes bolted to the walls over a panel of switches, and to my horror they were belting out hot air, dragged in from elsewhere. Actually roasting that underground space and making it even worse than it had to be. And I just demanded "Why?" of the whole goddamn world right then. "Why so goddamn hot down here?"

"Think fast," was what I thought Doctor Fell said, and I flinched back like someone was going to throw a dodgeball at me. And now I think I misheard just a little. I think she said, "To think fast." Because of time, you know? Because of how time must be, if you don't have a regular body temperature to keep you on the level. The thought hurt my head. The things you never think to think.

"Doc?" I called. Because after that cryptic utterance, she'd gone silent.

"Keep talking, Jasmine," came that voice in my helmet—I had to put the helmet on to hear it over the fans. To my left, off the fan room, were a row of ruined spaces. I could see the wreckage of tanks, the shattered glass glinting here and there in the silt of the floor, turned by the flow of the water. I wondered if that was where the green people had been born.

"What do you want to do now?" Doctor Fell asked me.

"Go home," I said, but then I said, "I want to see you." And it was to get her on side, right? Just to stop her telling her green children to stick me full of arrows. But it was true, too. I admit it. I wasn't signing on to whatever maniac scheme she had, but… tell me you wouldn't have been curious, in my place. "Tell me," I asked her. "What's it for, now? It can't all be *because it's there* anymore. Because it's already there. You've been there, done that. So why stick around? It can't be congenial here, no matter how you've got your crib set up."

"You think I'm missing the cut and thrust of debate with my peers?" she asked.

"Well, aren't you? Missing *something*, at least? You've been here twenty *years*. Being Queen of the Green People. Cut off on your island." And yes, still not an island, but they had me doing it by then. Imagining her surrounded by her beast-people creations. *That is the law*.

"You overestimate how cut off we are," she said, and something about the way she said it chilled me. I mean, not literally. I was overheating like fuck. But… glee. I heard glee and I didn't like it. And I could see the ducting for all the fan units—just stapled to the concrete walls like everything else—and it came from *down*, not up. You understand?

And anyway, that was when I heard the movement. Scared me to fuck. Sudden rush of feet. Thought it was the green men come to skin me, right? But no, that was when—

GLASSHOWER: That was when we came in.

PARNALLOV: And lucky for you we did. You'd have just walked in, would you?

GLASSHOWER: Crisis, please.

PARNALLOV: You'd have got your head on a stick.

GLASSHOWER: Crisis.

MARKS: Would I? Only, they could have killed me at any time.

GLASSHOWER: So, would you?

MARKS: What?

GLASSHOWER: Would you have gone over to her? That sounds as though it's where the conversation was going, doesn't it? Doctor Elaine Fell recruits her former protégée.

MARKS: If she'd wanted that, she had my social media contacts all this time for twenty years. I'm here because *you* recruited me, not her—wait, did you pick *me* because you thought she'd try it?

PARNALLOV: For a science nerd, she sure is slow on the uptake.

GLASSHOWER: Crisis, please. Doctor Marks, I won't insult you by trotting out the corporate party line. I hope you can understand we're facing a serious, perhaps an unprecedented situation here in the HDR.

MARKS: Because someone's been spending your research budget behind your back for twenty years.

CHELLER: (*laughs*)

GLASSHOWER: Something funny, Cheller?

CHELLER: Put me on this many meds, everything's funny, boss.

GLASSHOWER: Hmm. To answer your question, Doctor Marks, no. It's because this has been going on and it *hasn't* been tapping anyone's research budget, that we can work out. Doctor Fell and whatever accomplices have been doing their thing for twenty years under cover of these trees, and until very recently we had no idea. In fact, we're only here because the cycle of corporate attention swung back and people started asking if we couldn't use the Region for some commercial purposes again. Leading to a few flyovers and satellite attention. Leading to some anomalies and a trail of investigations. Leading to us, here.

PARNALLOV: Leading to a lot of good men and women getting killed. And if you say 'omelette, eggs' once more, you son of a bitch, I will pistol whip you.

(*pause*)

GLASSHOWER: I've apologised for that, Crisis. Heat of the moment.

PARNALLOV: You ain't got no 'heat of the moment' in you, you snake bast—

GLASSHOWER: (*speaking over him*) Be that as it *may*. We at least agree we have a job to do here. We can have this out at the debrief.

PARNALLOV: Fucking Debrief. Elhomey, report.

ELHOMEY: No movement out here. Or nothing I can see.

GLASSHOWER: If I can—

PARNALLOV: Come on down, then. Just watch the stairs.

GLASSHOWER: If I can—

PARNALLOV: Oh, no, all fucking yours.

GLASSHOWER: Doctor Marks—

MARKS: Why aren't you dead?

(*pause*)

GLASSHOWER: (*chuckles*) I'm sure there is some residual code of etiquette that should preclude the asking of that question. Where are they keeping your mentor, Doctor Marks? Where's her throne room, or prison cell, or life support pod or however it is that she ekes out her days here?

MARKS: I don't know. You grabbed me before I got to see her and hauled me back up here. She's down below. She must be. What are you going to... You're going to kill her, aren't you?

PARNALLOV: Fucking right we are.

GLASSHOWER: You've seen what she's accomplished.

MARKS: No. I mean, no. So she stayed on. So she saved the green people from being deleted like bad data. After which she's... stayed in the Zone, or she went back to the Zone, and she's... studied them, I guess. I mean it was all done before we got cut. Before she even came here, most of it. So you can't just... She's not done anything wrong. Or... Okay, she's done wrong things, but it's not like she's killed anyone. Or not her, herself. And, no, wait. You can't just... kill her. Like a hitman. I mean, you're not a hitman, Mr Glasshower.

(*pause*)

MARKS: Are you? Are you a hitman? Is that what you are?

(*pause*)

MARKS: What... what *are* you?

8.

ELHOMEY: —contact, sir.

GLASSHOWER: Veidt's node network?

ELHOMEY: No-o… it's… I'm not sure what network. We're
encrypted, though. Most likely someone knows we're
transmitting, but not what.

GLASSHOWER: Well, get me—

ELHOMEY: Blake?

GLASSHOWER: Doctor Blake, yes.

PARNALLOV: We should keep—

GLASSHOWER: Quiet. (*pause*) Crisis, you should know we're
most likely not getting out of this one.

MARKS: What?

PARNALLOV: Shut up.

GLASSHOWER: It's important, therefore, that we give the
outside world some idea of what we've found here, what the

situation is, don't you think?

MARKS: 'The outside world'?

PARNALLOV: I said shut up.

CHELLER: You mean Neosparan's board of directors, Max?

PARNALLOV: And you—!

GLASSHOWER: Well, I mean, first and foremost, but I really do mean the outside world. I mean the human race. I mean we have a problem, here, and I think we can deal with it, but if not...

BLAKE: (*distant*) Receiving now. Max, is that you? What the fuck is going on?

GLASSHOWER: Ah, good. Going to need you to keep a record of this, Doctor. We're in something of a bind.

ELHOMEY: Speaking of which, Marks is recording this right now.

GLASSHOWER: Well then do me a favour and turn her off, will you?

Session 40

IT'S JUST ME and him now.

He's prepping for a final one-man assault. I mean, one man and me, but I don't think I bring much to the equation.

He talked to Blake—that woman who was with him when I had my little job interview, who's running the operation back at Neosparan HQ. I'm sitting here thinking about that interview, where they sold me the line about the plane crash and all that, and considering just how staggeringly naïve I was at all times. How little I knew, yes, but that's fair enough. How little I even suspected, though. How few questions I asked. It was just a chance to get back to the Zone, to get back to that point in my life when I was relevant. To get back to Doctor Fell, who'd put me ever so briefly at the cutting edge.

I asked Glasshower if Doctor Fell killed Toby and Karim. I didn't even have to explain who I meant. He had all the details right there in his head. And all with that genial uncle act still, even though he's apparently some kind of assassin. Even though he's… something. Enough of a *something* that I tried to see if that grey hair—still somehow held in place by a king's ransom of product—was a wig, if the eyebrows would peel off, if he was one of *them* somehow gone rogue. And he said that, yes, almost certainly Toby and Karim were killed by Doctor Fell because they'd gone into the interior and seen too much of the main project. The green man project. And even then, I didn't feel that spike of hate and betrayal I should have. Like there's something cold-blooded about me, too.

I didn't want them to kill Doctor Fell. Crisis knew it. I think he probably told Glasshower that they should kill me before heading back down. Kill me, not because I knew too much, though I certainly knew too much. Kill me because they couldn't trust me to be on the right side. And suddenly it was sides. It was us versus the green men. I mean, it had been all along, ever since we came here to their place, but I mean *us* as in humans. Proper regular non-green humans.

"Isn't there some other way?" I asked. "I mean, we can't live in the Zone anyway. They're adapted for it. Why not just let them alone in peace? Diplomatic relations?"

I got the same look from all of them—Crisis, Cheller, Glasshower, Mayweather. Just... pitying. Just telling me I wasn't understanding the assignment. Cheller maybe a bit less, more of a shrug from them. Someone who went where their boss went because they were a good PA, not because they were actively invested in assassinating scientists and shutting down unauthorised experiments.

"Whatever's been done here," I tried, "the value to science..." Which, I admit, is never a good look when defending illicit human experimentation.

"We'll make sure to keep her notes," Glasshower threw out, again with a smile. Without so much as a sheen of sweat on his brow, although the rest of us were shiny with it, the red light glimmering from our skin like we were bioluminescing. Then we got going.

They were all armed—Glasshower, Crisis, Mayweather. I don't think Mayweather was a corporate killer by profession, genuinely just a tech, but she held a gun like someone who was used to it. Crisis gave Cheller his pistol, though they just clipped it to their belt. And then we suited up, because who knew what nastiness the green men could throw at us? They'd talked a lot about that environmental control room I'd seen, which was heating up the already stifling air. If the green men could adjust the dial, then we could get wet-bulb temperatures down here really suddenly, and that would be bad. And on that subject, Crisis and Mayweather had some plans for that place.

"It'll be genocide," I told them, my final arrow. "A race of people. A new species. You want them all dead." We were moving by now, I should say, heading down, suited and booted and communicating through radio. My suit battery was sitting around thirty-five per cent, the colours of the font shading from yellow to orange in case I was innumerate.

"We do, yes," Glasshower agreed equably.

"Genocide," I pressed.

"Are they a *gen*, though? The UN courts have been debating that one for a while. A new species created artificially, what rights does it have, exactly? I mean, if your governed region prohibits certain treatment of mammals, or vertebrates, or even people, does that extend to some unnatural species created in the laboratory, rather than the natural order?"

"Yes," I said promptly. "Because the laws are about the suffering, not taxonomy."

He shrugged. "What if you make it so they can't suffer? Though I accept that a lot of testing is precisely to see *how* things suffer, so that real people don't have to suffer later. But what if? Like that book with the meat that wants to be eaten, hm?" Again that ridiculously disarming grin. "I mean, it's a puzzler, don't get me wrong. All tied up in committees, currently. Will be for years. And nobody needs know what we did here, when it's done."

"I'll know," I said, stupidly.

Crisis snickered nastily—I wasn't doing anything for my life expectancy. Glasshower put a hand on my shoulder, weirdly sympathetic like he always was. "You won't tell," he said. "When it's done. When Doctor Fell has been appropriately corrected. Because we'll be the only game in town, then. We'll have her notes, and we'll revisit her Book of Genesis with all the appropriate safeguards that she and her predecessors never cared about. And you can be part of that, and put your education to proper use. That's what you want, I know. And through us—*only* through us—you can have it. You know that's how the Book of Genesis—the Bible one—works, right? Something so many people conveniently overlook is that God makes the world *twice* in the first few chapters: two different ways, different details."

I think we all gave him a blank look on that one but, given the suits and helmets, I can only vouch for me.

Down on the floor below, with the first set of dead labs, I pointed out that nobody was growing the green men here *now*. What did they think Doctor Fell was doing, exactly?

"There are deeper labs," Glasshower said casually. Mayweather was just coming back, having scouted as far as the next stairs. "In fact, I'm sure there are. Because something down there needs a lot of cooling." At my interrogative noise he said, "Why else pump hot air up, unless you've got, say, a room full of processing power they need to keep running at an optimal rate? Materials printers, artificial wombs, things like that."

I stopped, and Cheller bumped me from behind, the pistol in their belt jabbing me in the waist. I hadn't thought. Glasshower was way ahead of me.

Mayweather was out of sight, exploring, plumbing the depths, but her voice came clear over the radio. "You think they *need* the vats anymore? Or they just breed. I mean, the point of human genemods has always been heritability. For the space boys, anyway. Multigeneration zero-G and exoplanet missions, build a human for any habitat, right? That was Jun's deal."

"The universe can be considered an exercise in wildly fluctuating temperature gradients," Glasshower pronounced. "From the heart of a star to the vacuum of space. In which natural humans function at only a range of a handful of degrees before our bodies fail. Yes, I think you're right. This is a cancerous outgrowth of the space genemod program. So we must strive to save the notes. Perhaps there'll be a planet out there that Doctor Fell's creations will find more congenial than we will. Perhaps we will need to recreate them. But first we need to destroy them."

"Why?" I demanded.

"Jesus, she still doesn't get it," Crisis said. "Mayweather, you see any of them yet?"

"If they're down here with us, then they're keeping out of sight," came her voice. "I thought Jasmine said she saw them."

"I *thought* I saw them," I said, and then, "I'm not sure what I saw, now. It's the light."

"It doesn't make things easy," Glasshower admitted.

And then the new voice, breaking in on our radio channel. "I suppose I should say welcome. Give you the tour. Show you the gift shop."

"Elaine? Elaine Fell?" Glasshower queried. "I recognise that voice, I think."

"Fucking *encryption*," Crisis growled, presumably at Mayweather,

"You should stop what you're doing and walk away," Doctor Fell's voice said pleasantly.

"You've made it way too personal for that," said Crisis.

"You came here to kill me and destroy all my work," she told him. "I feel it was already personal."

Glasshower chuckled like he was about to make two fighting children make up and shake hands. "She's got us there, Crisis. But what work, Elaine? I mean you've been here undercover for twenty years, and, what, ten before that, at most? That's a long stint of research, but not so much for development of something like this. We've seen your 'work' and it's obviously good—got a real close look at the guts of it outside. But they must be first generation, right? Still experimental, fresh out of the vats. Probably not even a breeding population yet. Just a mistake. So maybe you agree that this sort of work should take place in a properly controlled and funded way with peer review and safety protocols, and not this HG Wells BS, and come back with us. I mean this business probably qualifies you for going up in front of the UN courts or something, but we're all grown-ups. We can overlook a few foibles where someone's been sociopathic in a usefully clever way. You can be the Wernher von Braun of genetic modification. Just let us put your prototypes back in the box." And I know he said these exact words because, even though they weren't letting me record the radio right then, I could record me, just plain me, on another channel. I was muttering along with them all, trying to parrot exactly what was said. In case it was evidence in some big trial later—Fell's trial, or Glasshower's.

And Doctor Fell laughed in a way that made me shiver. "You think that, do you? That they're all wet behind the ears, my people? But, Max, haven't you thought that perhaps this place isn't *my* work? I just took it over after the funding died, but they'd had two generations of the finest minds working on the problem. Reclaiming the Zone for humanity. Except that isn't quite how it went. Not quite."

"We should Agent Orange this whole goddamned jungle from the air," Crisis broke in. Everyone, as far as I can tell, ignored him.

"And even that's an assumption. That what you're seeing here *is* just a chance breakthrough, someone writing a sequel to the Human Genome Project. Just regular mad scientist stuff, Frankenstein stops for a roadside picnic. Don't you think they might have been there before? In the shrinking jungles, staring out at the cattlemen and the timbermen. Beneath still waters. You've heard about the aquatic ape theories, surely."

"Enough to know they're BS," agreed Glasshower cheerily. "I'm not buying what you're selling, Elaine. Not if you're telling me the Creature from the Black Lagoon is moving in next door all of a sudden."

"Really? But haven't you heard? We're in a collapsing climate disaster. The Zone's just one part of it. Collapsing as in, all our usable biomes crunching together as the heat pushes out from the equator. And you've all seen how that goes. Everything wants to live. People move north and south, animals move north and south, diseases move north and south. Waves of epidemics as all those people and animals and microbes mix in new configurations. Every year a new wave of hospitalisations from some fresh plague that's mutating to survive the conditions *we're* imposing on the world. A new invasive species that eats our lawns and flowers and the crops we need to survive. Ancient breeds unseen for millions of years now driven from the deepest tropics into your very backyard. And so they come. Are they really *new*, Max? Or are they very, very old?"

There was a silence, a few beats of thought after that. I remember Cheller was clutching at my arm and it was more than just their leg or the fatigue.

"BS," said Glasshower. "Bee. Ess. A good spook show for the tourists, but I've seen the patents on half of this."

And then there was a shout from Crisis and a scatter of gunfire down on the floor below.

"Fucking *contact*," came his voice, and then, "Mayweather, report."

"I'm fine. I'm in cover," from her. "At least five of them. At least one with a gun."

"Just put an *arrow* a foot into the wall," Crisis said, sounding like it was through clenched teeth. "Hold tight. I'm coming to you."

"Covering you," Mayweather told him.

Glasshower was heading down, his own gun half-raised. We took the stairs after him, Cheller stiff-legged despite the painkillers. My status, as team-mate or prisoner, seemed perpetually in flux.

Down below, we came to the larger open spaces I'd found. Ahead, the rumble of the fans shook the air and my suit readouts told me how the temperature was going up. Even as I saw it, Crisis said, "Got eyes on the control room. Mayweather?"

"Ready."

"Glasshower?"

"Ready, Crisis. Go get 'em."

A lot of things happened very quickly, then, and I don't know if I really understood them enough at the time to recount them now, but I'll do my best. Because it was the last I saw of most of the people there.

There was gunfire ahead, from the direction of the control room. Through the helmet it came out as dull popping, like a string of streamers at a disappointing party. We were down on that level now, the three of us. Glasshower ahead, turning to me, and I saw *VEIDT* on his helmet for the first time and felt a sick lurch in my stomach. Because of course his own had been broken by the arrow—*that he had somehow survived*—and he'd apparently scavenged Oskar's corpse for a replacement on the way in. Had probably been right behind Cheller and me when we were escorted in here. Hadn't stepped in to help Oskar, just come after like a vulture to take the man's kit.

Then they were on us. They came from behind, from upstairs, from outside. Which, somehow, none of us had thought of. Possibly Cheller or Glasshower was supposed to be keeping an eye out, in Crisis's tactical map of the situation, but everyone had been thinking *down* and *inwards* and that we had the enemy bottled up in here, when of course they were all around us.

I remember Cheller just being ripped from beside me, flung away. Bodies pushing past me, swift and purposeful. Glasshower swinging the gun barrel round in an arc that absolutely included me, but then they were on him and I was running. Running away, floundering in the suit, going after Crisis and Mayweather because that was somehow safer than staying where I was despite the bullets in the air over there. And ending up in the environment room, seeing Crisis there just before they got him. He was at the bank of controls, and I very obviously sold him short when I cast him as the bluff, simple military man hired to shoot people. He'd grokked the system right away, or else Mayweather had given him instructions. And it was big and mechanical, not lots of screens and readouts and password authentication. Robust and reliable tech, to survive the Zone.

The arrow went right through him. Actually that sounds like I saw it go in. It was just… *in* him, though, where a moment before there had been no arrow, like a bad special effect, like a magic trick. Pinning him to the metal of the control panel for a moment before he slumped back and pulled the tip free. I saw one of the green men at the doorway holding… not a bow, actually. A thing like a crossbow without the *cross*, or a cartoon rifle. A box with a shoulder stock, basically, and a big hole the arrow had come out of. Pneumatic or something. Not your Robin Hood business.

"Fucker," said Crisis conversationally in my ear. "Take this, you cold-blooded son of a bitch." And whatever he'd been doing at the panel was apparently finished, because he yanked down one more lever and suddenly all the hot air left the room and the temperature plummeted, ridiculously fast. I have no idea what was below, in terms of heating and cooling systems, but it was industrial scale. Frost started forming in a heartbeat. The water—the inches of water that had been migrating across the floor, running down the walls—it froze. My suit display started displaying all kinds of warnings about *low* temperature, all of which were surplus to requirements right then. The air glittered with tiny frozen particles.

Crisis chuckled, slumped awkwardly against the wall, the arrow forcing his body into an unnatural pose. "Catch cold, fucker," he said. I saw his gloved hands move slowly, gingerly, reaching for the shaft of the arrow. The whine of his suit's fans was audible as a high scream over the thunder of the room, because its integrity was compromised and it was still trying to keep him warm enough to stay alive.

I should say, I was on my knees, and they had frozen to the floor. I was fighting to get myself unstuck without ripping my suit. Battery power at twenty-six per cent, said my display.

I looked at the green man with the arrow-shooting weapon, expecting to find them a heap on the ground. They were shivering, their muscles jumping like they were being electrocuted. Generating *heat*. They stood still, and then they started to move. I think I was watching the changeover, one set of proteins taking over from another, manufactured and sent to the front line with hellish speed. Their every motion was exaggeratedly slow and deliberate, like something from a nightmare. I watched as they drew another arrow from the quiver slung from a shoulder strap. It was all of a piece, plastic from head to flights. I remembered Glasshower saying they had a printer below, and those arrows were how he'd known. Nobody was pissing about with the Middle Ages around here. Possibly it was harder to fabricate a chemical propellant than just make a really powerful airgun.

I watched as the green man's hands moved with exquisite slowness, slotting the missile into the barrel of the weapon. Their voice came to me like a slow drone, as though they were half asleep.

"It's not so easy," they drawled, "to get rid of us. Heat won't. Cold won't. We just speed up. We just slow down. They made us to live."

Crisis was trying to get his rifle, but it was frozen in the half-inch of ice on the ground. I could hear him wheezing over the radio. I was thinking about protein isoforms and over-engineering. Or else Doctor Fell wasn't gaslighting Glasshower after all, and these were some ur-humans from the dawn of time, come back to take the planet out of the hands of their irresponsible cousins. A survival from that age when our ancestors were just one of many possible definitions of the word 'human.' And I didn't believe it for a moment. They were gene-tech, sure enough.

Except there really *had* been multiple species of humans once, and now there were again, and there are multiple ways that a thing can be true.

I got my knees free, slithered and slipped and staggered. The green man was advancing on Crisis in a terrible slow-motion stalk, like they wanted him to appreciate the careful movement of every muscle. Barefoot on the ice, step after deliberate step. Crisis was trying to pry the gun free, but he didn't have the strength, and the arrow shaft kept getting in the way. He got a knife out, after that. I was expecting a pistol, but he'd given that to Cheller, of course. The green man stopped outside his reach.

"You won't beat us," Crisis said quietly. "Green fuckers sitting here in your jungle. We'll bury you in white phosphorus. Humans will win. Always do."

"Yes," the green man said, the words dragging out lugubriously. "Humans always win." Like Cro Magnon man and a Neanderthal meeting sixty thousand years ago.

I tried to get in the way, then. I had the idea that I could stand between them and, somehow, be too valuable to just kill. Ignoring the fact that arrow could go right through me on its way to its intended recipient. I was so cold, though. Despite the suit's best efforts, my teeth were chattering and my mammal body was doing all the debilitating things it does to try and keep its temperature up within survivable levels. And I fell over on the ice—on my back. Felt the light-drinker plates crack, not that they were doing me much good. And I missed when the arrow actually flew. Only that Crisis was dead, a second shaft standing proud between his collarbones. And the green man's head slowly turning towards me, looking at me with those eyes. *Click… click.* A green *woman*, I realised. Almost no breasts, almost no difference, but I think she was a woman. Then she was going step after lagging step towards the controls—not a plod, but as though she was a dancer told to move as slowly as possible. A ballet of slow-motion cinematography.

Then there were hands on me. Quick hands. Glasshower, his gun slung, bundling me away, lurching and skidding but compensating each time. I didn't fight him. He didn't pull me back the way we'd come, but further in. A man with a mission.

We've stopped in a room with almost no light. Glasshower is trying to raise the others, I think. Cheller and Mayweather.

Nothing from either of them, so it's a one-man assault. I said he should leave me behind, and he gave me a look—he had his helmet off, so I saw it clear. That look said he wouldn't be taking me along as backup, but as bargaining chip or human shield. And still with a smile, like I was a child and hadn't quite understood the rules of the game we'd all been playing. And that, I think, was the point of me being here. I wasn't the expert, after all. They'd all known far more than I had about what was going on here, right from the start. I was just leverage. A lever now being turned into a blunt instrument.

"Neosparan," I said to him just now, "has some weird criteria they look for in a manager."

"Let's just say they didn't bring me on board for my administrative skills," he agreed. And then: "Well, it looks like nobody else is coming to the party." A bright look at me. "It has to be done," he said. "Now. Before they spread. You said, why not just let them have the Zone? You saw, just now. We made them too well. They could live barefoot in Antarctica." I don't know if that *we* meant humanity, or if his employer actually had a hand in it and is trying to clean up its inconveniently spilled lab experiment. He looks… tired, actually. Human. Someone with a nasty job that nobody else was going to do. Nobody's hero, but nobody's monster.

"Elaine?" he asked, over our channel. "Doctor Fell, you're still there, I'm sure."

"I am following your adventures with great interest, Max," came her voice.

"And yet you've not sent your flying monkeys to carry us off just yet," Glasshower noted. "Which suggests I have something of value to you. Nice that the mentor-student bond persists for so long. What say I bring Jasmine here to you?" He's laid out a handful of magazines, counted and then re-stowed them, like some sort of prayer or ritual.

"Come on in," Doctor Fell's voice agreed. "The water's lovely."

9.

Session 41

UNKNOWN: —sshower? You there?

GLASSHOWER: Who's speaking, please? I'm afraid I'm somewhat engaged at the moment.

UNKNOWN: (*static*) —are you?

GLASSHOWER: Elaine, you appear to be having technical difficulties.

UNKNOWN: It's Elhomey. Mayweather Elhomey. What the hell happened to you?

GLASSHOWER: Mayweather?

ELHOMEY: Right. Where did you all go? I can't raise Crisis.

GLASSHOWER: That would be on account of him being dead. Where are you? Is Cheller with you?

ELHOMEY: No. I'm down a level. In a… cupboard, basically. (*pause*) Dead. Christ, this is a mess.

GLASSHOWER: Well, I'm just about to mop it up. We're
   descending to your level now. Jasmine and myself. Any
   company I should know about?
ELHOMEY: They are all over the place. I'm coming to you.

Session 42

So...

   In what time I have before...

   This is how it ends.

   Mayweather met us, like she said. The standard hazard
suits—they're in various shades of grey, but somehow they
leapt out at me in that red light, even as the green men vanished
into every shadow. I was feeling very claustrophobic right then,
so many levels down, sloshing through knee-deep water that
was *still* rushing away to some abyss even further beneath us.
How far did they *dig* to build this place? Surely we didn't go so
far *up* from the river that we're not way *below* the water table
now, so how is the water still going *down?* How many levels
does the place even have? It's a warren. A hive, rather. Warrens
are for cute bunnies, after all. But right then the sight of that
hazard suit, the name *ELHOMEY* on the brow of the helmet,
that was infinitely reassuring. We were three, then. And I had
hope that Cheller had made it somehow. I hadn't seen their
body. Even though this tomb of a place seemed exactly the
right spot for people to vanish into, no bodies and no traces.
Stories never told.

   I think we only found Karim and Toby's bodies because they

wanted us to. Because tying off their stories with a fiction of failed suits was neater, leading to fewer questions and search parties. They could have just disappeared into the jungle. The two of them, the laughing boys. Keen postgrads who just wanted to *know* and to build careers for themselves. Minds like gifts for the future to unwrap, and then they died. They'd tried to persuade me to come along. *It's all being shut down anyway. We're done here. Why not go peek?* And they found out why not, and if I'd been persuaded away from composing my final report, I'd have found out too. Found the secret of the Zone twenty years earlier and then died from it. Or maybe they just died, without ever finding out anything at all. Like the people in the tent. At least I know, now. At least, if they're going to kill me, I've found out this much.

We saw a lot down here. Space leading off in all directions. A factory floor area big as an aircraft hangar. Impossibly vast, except in this light it was hard to say, hard for the eye to really get a handle on perspective. We found the laboratories. Enough to know they aren't being born out of vats anymore. Aren't reliant on the constant mediation of science to produce little green babies. If they ever had been. And I don't believe Doctor Fell's spook stories about atavisms and ancient strands of humanity or inhumanity or whatever, but that doesn't mean they're not true. I've gone so far beyond what I know, now, that what I believe has become a matter of personal whim, not external evidence.

It's cold down here. Not actually air-condition cold, but almost hospitable. The rooms with the working kit had raised floors and the air was drier, even though there was water coursing across every floor. The grumble of the fans underscored every sound and echo of the place. They needed it cooler to keep the machines running. The research station's existing systems have been repurposed. Glasshower commented on what a busy little monster Doctor Fell had been since she came back.

The printers were top of the range. That gave us all pause. They could make a lot of things with those machines. Not just arrows and spearguns, but all sorts. Molecular-level printing. Medicines, drugs, poisons. There was kit there that I think was for gene-editing, though I don't think they could play build-a-bear with a whole human genome anymore. You could probably create a novel microorganism, though. And that in itself was heavily prescribed, because right now we had enough difficulty dealing with successive waves of *naturally* mutated viruses without someone making new ones.

I think Glasshower and I were having the same grim thoughts, looking at all that kit. I half expected him to start smashing it up, but that would have brought them down on us sooner, and he had a mission. Cut the head off the snake.

And I was seeing the green people all the time, by then. Or maybe I was. The space was big enough, the light dim enough—and in the red light their *green* only ever looked grey anyway, blending with every surface and shade. Every shadow held a watching figure, until you moved close enough or flicked your torch at it. They watched us from wherever you didn't look. The hairs on my mammal body were pricking against the inside of my hazard suit, screaming their proximity at me.

"Their eyes," I said, "must be better. In this light. Better at the red end of the spectrum."

Glasshower grunted an affirmative, then added, "Thankfully, so are mine."

That seemed unfair, and I remember Mayweather turning, her visor staring at him. Then we found another set of stairs, but saw they were flooded entirely, halfway down. Whatever lower reaches of the base existed, they were drowned. I don't know if that's even an impediment to the green men. I saw fish down there, pallid in the beam of my torch. Snakes squirming to get away from my scrutiny.

My suit battery said nineteen per cent and the number was helpfully set in red to focus me. I didn't raise that with the others. They must have been in the same boat.

When we turned from the sunken stairs, they were there. Three green people: I think two women and a man, but it was hard to say. And Cheller.

Cheller's helmet was off, but down in that cool it was probably more congenial for them than their captors. A green man held their wrist; with that injured leg they'd not be haring off anywhere. The green people moved slowly, deliberately. *Click-click* went their eyes, which kept staring at us through those slow blinks.

"Interesting," said Glasshower. He had his gun half-levelled, as did Mayweather. I, of course, had no gun. I wouldn't have known what to do with one. My family were never gun-havers. We were naturalised immigrants. We weren't ever white enough for our neighbours to be happy with us exercising our second-amendment rights.

Doctor Fell's voice came to us over our radios. "Glad to see you finally made it, Max."

"I'm just recasting myself," came Glasshower's easy reply. "Didn't realise we were playing at hostage exchange." He was still on the move, cutting a curving path around the big space, watching the green people pivoting lazily to follow him. Cheller looked… tired, swaying. They'd still be pumped full of painkillers, but they looked as though they'd just drop if one more thing happened to them. Their eyes followed Glasshower's progress mutely.

And I tried to stay still, but now Glasshower's hand was on my elbow, gentle until I didn't go with him and then like a vice. Mayweather shadowed me, and it seemed her gun was pointing at me as much as at the green people. Suddenly I was a prisoner again, a hostage, fit for exchange.

"I don't know how much you value this one, to be honest," Doctor Fell said. "They say they've been on your staff for years, Watson to your Holmes, but they have an obvious motive to make me think they're valuable enough to keep around."

"I am very fond of Cheller," Glasshower confirmed, almost absently, not looking at his PA. We'd been moving along one concrete wall of the underground space, but halfway through Doctor Fell's words, he'd stopped. The green people had shifted, moved one lethargic step towards him. One of them had a speargun like the one that had killed Crisis, and now it was pointed at him, much as his gun was pointed at them. Because of the door.

There were plenty of doorways, yes. They stood open, like denuded sockets. Nobody here had much need of privacy, it seemed, just like the green men wore nothing but a few scraps. Except there was one door. An actual door, and closed. So normal a thing, but it stood out like a scream precisely because nothing else was normal.

"Well, one of us has to say it," Glasshower said. "I had hoped Jasmine here might be of some sentimental value to you. Old times' sake, you know. For what it's worth, I think she has a lot of residual loyalty to *you*. You were obviously quite the inspiration."

"I offered her a chance at significance, building the future," Doctor Fell told us in our ears. "I'm sorry I couldn't bring her with me. Reaching out would have been too much of a risk. But she's here now, and I can always use disciples."

Glasshower had been very still, listening, and I had, too, because I'd finally caught up. I couldn't hear what he heard, though, not with the fans and the echoes. Glasshower had, though; I could tell from how he held himself. He had better ears, along with everything else. I guessed, even then, that he'd heard an extra voice. One speaking along with the Doctor Fell in our ears: the sound of the actual Doctor Fell in the next room.

"You want me to exchange your former research student for my personal assistant? There's a sentence you never thought you'd have to say," he remarked. His stance was very casual, the gun barrel actually dipping towards the floor. His extreme tension came to me through his fingers, still pincering my arm.

"I have uses for her," Doctor Fell confirmed. "And your person Friday here has been upselling their usefulness to you. I mean, you wouldn't want to have to organise your *own* appointments, would you?"

Glasshower pulled his helmet fully back, letting it rock between his shoulder blades. Underneath, he was still immaculately styled. I took this as a cue to do the same, saving a little battery life. The cool of the space hit me, like waking up. Mayweather kept hers on, of course.

"How are you doing, Cheller?" Glasshower called. "Treated appropriately as an enemy combatant, as per the relevant conventions?" I thought about when he'd been talking about the green people as not a *gen* that could be *-ocided*. Outside all such rules and protections.

"Coping," Cheller said weakly. "Keen to be back in the office, if I'm honest."

"Yes, well," Glasshower said. And then: "Yes, well, let's get it over with. Here's Doctor Jasmine Marks, mostly intact. She's signed a lot of NDAs with Zeisuritan and Neosparan, so I hope you weren't expecting her to disclose any trade secrets."

"Before we conclude our business," came Doctor Fell's voice, and that time I caught it. As well as the voice from the radio—a little softer, now I'd pushed my helmet back—the faint rumble of a live person speaking just on the far side of that door. The one door, a symbol of rank and significance. The Office of Doctor Moreau. "I have a question for you. Out of scientific curiosity."

"I'm flattered. I rather feel the balance of scientific questions should be going the other way," Glasshower replied, "but do ask."

"What are you, Max? Because you're not really human, are you? A human would be dead twice over, in your shoes."

"Well, in my defence, they're very expensive shoes," he said, and then glanced at me, as though enquiring whether I, too, wanted to know. Which I did, frankly, although right then I was too scared of him and everything else to say it. "I'm the alternative," he explained. "To all this nonsense. I'm the real way we'll walk on other worlds and survive whatever the Earth throws at us. None of this noble savage tomfoolery, this freakshow of yours. No offence." He offered a companionable nod to the impassive green faces. "Implants, mostly. Cooling my blood, conducting heat. Better retinas, better ears, improved reflexes. Proper science, Elaine. Human science, done by humans to humans to make them superhuman. Not this. Never this Innsmouth BS you keep getting your hands dirty with. I'd say you should come help us, but it's not your field and you're too invested in this. It's a shame. You were brilliant. Before you fell off the map. What I *am* is the future. Humanity's future. The bespoke one, rather than your breeding masses. How did you do the alligators, by the way? That's my own final question. I assume we didn't just happen to arrive for Reptile Pride or something."

"They're the nastiest predators in the Zone," Doctor Fell said equably. "Being semi-aquatic means they can get huge and not overheat. So we had to work out some pheromonal means of repelling them. Which turns into controlling and herding them remarkably easily. I thought you'd appreciate the show."

"Impressive but misguided, as always," said Glasshower. "I think that concludes the Q-and-A section of today's event. Shall we get on with the gift-giving? I didn't get a chance to wrap yours." I still remember—I still find it hard to reconcile—

the difference between those blithe words and the incredible tension in his grip. Desperation. The hero in the dragon's lair, seeing the kindle of its eyes in the dark. But knowing this was *it,* his chance to slay it. To sever the head of the serpent. He didn't spare the green people a glance, really. Nobody goes to the Island just to exterminate the beast-people. Nobody just kills the dragon's young and breaks the eggs. Glasshower knew he would get one chance to complete his mission and rid the world of the threat that was Doctor Elaine Fell, and this was it. And I could have said something. I could have shouted a warning. Not that it would have changed much, but...

He gave me a push and I staggered a couple of steps towards them, realising nobody had asked me what I actually *wanted*, and that I didn't, in fact, know. Obviously I didn't want to end up in the hands of the dreadful green people. Obviously I did want to be reunited with Doctor Fell, to continue important work, to be a part of the Big Secret that had been going on here since before I first arrived, and which had continued after I left. And only now, somehow, did I click to the third side of that syllogistic triangle: that these two desires were mutually exclusive.

Cheller was released by their own captors. We crossed. A prisoner exchange, exactly like the man had said. An exchange of looks, too. Mutual sympathy. A pair of pawns without any agency in what was going on.

Green hands reaching for me. And the slowness of them, the languorous underwater pace of their graceful movements, it was like a nightmare. And, like a nightmare, I couldn't make myself run away.

They turned me towards the door, pulled me, not the sudden yank of energetic metabolisms, but a slow, building strength that was still more than I could resist. Alien touch and alien motion, slow and irresistible as tree roots. Towards the door. That normal, normal thing that had suddenly become the focus of all horror in the buried world.

I decided I did not want to do this after all. I came down very abruptly on the side of *not* being given over to the green men, now it was too late to stop it happening. I twisted in their stone-like grip, turned to stare at Glasshower, to make some plea. I saw him move.

He was so swift. They had been ready for him, the speargun raised, but he was too fast. I never saw anyone move so fast. The spear caught poor Cheller instead, transfixed them through the chest. That asinine little joke about being back in the office, that was the last thing they ever said. All I could think was how we'd none of us realised, as they said it, and how they'd surely have said something better if they'd known.

Glasshower, though. He was at us and through us before I had a chance to register it. I got an elbow to the chest and the green people who held me were knocked down like skittles. I heard his voice shouting at Mayweather to do something— probably to shoot the green people, maybe me as well. Then he had the door open, his gun coming up to encompass the demise of Doctor Fell. And he'd die after that, he knew, but it wouldn't matter. To him the Zone was a hothouse flower, and once he'd severed the life-giving root it would wither and die.

He stopped. I heard him make an odd little noise, over the whine of the fans. It sounded like a laugh.

"Sorry, Max," came Doctor Fell's voice, clearly audible in that relative quiet.

The arrowhead was abruptly sticking out of the small of his back, but it was the gun that killed him. A line of bullets that went *pock-pock-pock* into the concrete wall and then played join-the-dots across his shoulder blades in little explosions of blood red and bone white and then went on to trace a rising curve of dents in the wall on the other side of the door.

Mayweather lowered her gun. Or, rather, the person wearing Mayweather's suit lowered Mayweather's gun. I was with Cheller then, trying to… do something. Help, somehow. Too late. They were already gone, and Glasshower was gone, and presumably Mayweather was long gone, murdered in the dark around the same time as Crisis was getting his. I thought about how swiftly 'Mayweather' had acted, but then the suits could keep you warm as easily as cool. If you were a green man in need of a boosted metabolism, then modern technology was there for you.

I stood up from Cheller's corpse and found myself drawn, step by unwilling step, to that open doorway. Eyes straying to the bullet holes either side of it. To the body propping the door open. To the figure inside.

There was a terminal in there, multiple screens, all slightly outdated, showing a variety of windows and applications. More fans bolted to the wall. A bunk. A room entirely lacking in Doctor Fell. One green woman there, her speargun reloaded.

"I suppose Max wasn't the future after all," she said, in the tones of Doctor Fell. "Just an evolutionary dead end. A failed spur of the human family tree." And she smiled at me, or at least made her face into the shape of a smile by obvious, deliberate effort. Her teeth were quite human, not the shark's rack I had half expected. The voice was so perfect that I almost thought it was actually *her*, surgically altered beyond any other recognition. Then I caught up: the way her lips had moved, but the sound had come from further into the room, directly behind her. The terminal.

"Her voice," I said stupidly.

"Technology," said her voice, to the motion of the green woman's lips.

"Then where is she?" I demanded, still stupidly. "Where are you keeping her. Doctor Fell? Doctor Fell!" Standing there over Glasshower's body, shouting out the name of my mentor like a lost child calling for mother.

"She's dead, Jasmine," she said, and probably she hadn't thought—she was just still linked to the emulator—but the continued use of Elaine Fell's voice felt like cruelty. "She's been dead for almost fourteen years."

"You killed her," I accused.

"No, but she died," I was told. "Life here is hard for your kind. You know that."

"You killed her like you killed everyone. Like you killed Toby and Karim." Two names she didn't even recognise, and besides, if my fellow students had been killed by the green people back then, did I really think it hadn't been at Doctor Fell's orders? But I was collapsing. Not physically but mentally. All the walls coming down before the tidal wave. "You think you've won!" I shouted at them all. "You haven't won anything. People won't let you live, you know that? They already know, outside. Glasshower called them. Called Doctor Blake from his office. There'll be another expedition. It'll be ready for you. Or—no, Crisis was right. They'll just napalm this whole place from the air. Won't even risk another person. Another human person. What'll you do? Shoot arrows at the planes? You can't win against *people*. They'll exterminate you." Staring at her expressionless face, at all their expressionless faces.

"And what do you think, about that?" dead Doctor Fell interpreted for the green people, conjured to brief life by the mime of the green woman.

I stared at her, at them, and said, "I don't know."

"We have some cleaning up to do," said Doctor Fell's ghost from the terminal. "You need somewhere quiet to collect your thoughts. We'll come back for you, after. To decide what to do."

And here I am, in a quiet room that might have been anything, once, but is now just some rotting rags and fungus on the walls and the world's shallowest indoor swimming pool. There are geckos down here, and centipedes, and a variety of bugs both wall-based and aquatic. I've watched them in the dead, red light as I've recorded these, perhaps my last words. For... who? I don't know. But I've been keeping this record and it may as well be complete. RIP Maxwell Glasshower and Cheller and Mayweather Elhomey, and all the rest of them: Oskar, Jun, Crisis, Peter, Amy, Yusuf. Gorse, was that the sergeant's name? Was it? The others, whose names I can't even remember. My suit's now down to the dregs of its power, as though the weight of these, my last words, is too much for it to bear.

10.

BUT IT'S ALL right. They're letting me go now. I'm going home. Back to Zeisuritan. Back to my address. But before I embark, I shall tell you how it ended. This account should be complete, should it not?

They came and took me, back to the room with the door where Doctor Fell had seemed to be. The trick they'd played on Max. And on me. The bodies had gone, by then. They'd cleaned up.

There were three of them. Green men and women. Nearly naked. Savages, I thought, even though I'd had evidence to the contrary. And I was nearly naked too. They'd taken my suit. Taken it, and then left me alone for a long time with nothing but my own voice. I cried, left alone in the dark. They were always watching. I begged them. They gave me water—tasting flat from the filter—and fish. River fish, freshly caught. I choked on the bones, because I ate it too greedily. I made a lot of rash promises about what I would or wouldn't say if they let me go back home, what I would or wouldn't do for them. I'd conceal them. I'd protect them. And they didn't ask anything of me, in the end. No Devil's bargain with the green people for Jasmine Marks. Jasmine Marks just gets to go home, sole survivor.

I threatened them with the wrath of Neosparan and Doctor Blake, too, and they just looked at me and seemed to laugh amongst themselves without moving their lips.

When they took me, they brought me to that room with a door, and the screens were on, and the three people inside told me they were going to let me talk to the outside. Did I have complaints? I was free to make them. I treated it like a hostage situation. I asked them what they wanted. I was very willing to do what they wanted, I assured them. Though possibly I would have tried to mug out some kind of coded cry for help in amongst the collaboration. We'll never know. Instead, they told me there would be no need for any of that.

Doctor Blake came up on the screen. There were tears in my eyes. I started talking so fast, no real words came out. Just gabble. Doctor Blake regarded me calmly and I could see the Neosparan board room behind her, just like I'd seen when I was first recruited by her and Glasshower.

I said a lot of things to Doctor Blake. Things I should probably not have said, if I was at all worried about the company I was in and the fate I might meet for my loose lips. I burst out about how everyone was dead and there were green people and she, Doctor Blake, needed to get me out of there. And all the while Doctor Blake on the screen watched me and the three green people watched me, standing to either side so they were out of sight. A fine joke on me and Doctor Blake, to make me look mad and fool her into thinking there were no green men!

And eventually my words stopped, slowed to a trickle and then a drip, then nothing. And Doctor Blake stared at me, solemn. Not incredulous as I might have expected, but entirely professional, as befits a doctor. As solemn and serious as Doctor Fell ever was. And she leant forwards, closer and closer to her camera, until she was uncomfortably close. Too close. Face filling the screen. She was smiling just a little. A tiny, deliberate curl at the corners of her lips.

She blinked. *Click-click.*

I screamed and leapt back and hit the wall in a way that was painful. And stopped, like I'd stuck there. Staring.

"Yes," Doctor Blake said. "We are already here. I'm afraid Max's little murder mission was doomed from the start. Or, not murder. What's that edgy little slang that's so very apposite for your situation? Wetwork, is it?"

I spluttered and choked and had no words.

"Your mistake," said Vapella—one of the green people in the room with me—"was that you saw us as savages."

"Noble or otherwise," Doctor Blake added from the screen.

"You *are* savages!" I shouted at them rudely. "You murdered everyone! You murdered Toby and Karim. You murdered Doctor Fell!"

"Taking your accusations in order," Vapella said with great magnanimity, "if 'everyone' refers to the members of your expedition, then we plead self-defence, given that they were part of an effort to uncover and exterminate us. If 'Toby and Karim' refer to the staff members of the research team you were a part of, that was entirely the decision of Doctor Fell. And we did not kill Doctor Fell."

My face showed my sudden hope. "She's alive?"

"She died, as we said. This is not a good place for you," Vapella said. "But before she died, she helped us. She was not our maker, but she had come to believe in us. To want to preserve what we were. Not as slaves, not as subjects. As people."

"And this is how you repay us?" I shouted at them. They just looked at me, wanting me to see the whole history of it, to assemble it in my head. The human inhumanity to humans that must be buried in our genetic past, beyond even our ability to recall.

"What are you?" I demanded at last. The big question.

"We are the children of the monsters you created," said Vapella. "The monsters you made too well. We are the other humanity. The fittest, who will survive. We are the inheritors."

"You can't think you'll…" Again I stuttered over my words. "How many of you even are there?"

"Ask yourself that question and wonder," said Vapella. "In the Zone, many. Outside the Zone, many. Amongst you."

"But you're *green*," I said stupidly.

"It is an algae that lives within the top layer of our skin. It feeds us, a little. And we need only a little, not needing to run our body-fires so constantly. Needing *not* to, if we are to survive here. Cold-bloodedness is the best diet."

"The algae can be killed off and removed," said Doctor Blake. "The process is swift and painless, as I myself recall."

"What happened to the real Doctor Blake?" I demanded.

"Oh, I am she," she said. "In my case, Doctor Fell was able to create an identity for me, academic credentials. Which I more than qualify for, by the way. I earned another doctorate after I left the Zone. I am one of the longest-standing members of our community to find a place in the wider world."

"But you're... not human. You're *ectotherms*," I said, as though it was a rude word. "Reptiles. Snakes. Cold." All very undiplomatic.

"Once that might have been a disadvantage," Vapella admitted. "But not anymore, thanks to you."

"Me?" I said, still stupidly.

"All of you. *Homo sapiens homeothermus*. You have been very obliging in undoing all your own advantages," she explained. "You have warmed the world until far more of it is congenial to us than would otherwise have been the case. Do you know some scientists think we should be starting a new ice age around now? How terrible that would be! How slow we would become! But instead, you warm the world for us. You add energy to the global system for us, so that we can borrow it to keep our bodies warm and our minds swift. You melt the icecaps so there is more free water for us, to fill the hot, hot air until you cannot live in it. But *we* can. We live, and every day the world is more and more the way we like it. We bask in your warmth and our minds go swift and sure. And where we must go to cold places that would make us slow and unhappy, you already have your technology in place, so that we can make those places as warm as we like. A congenial habitat where we thrive, as invasive species often do. You have paved the way for us at every turn with the changes you have made to the world."

I looked horrified by all of this.

"Is it not better," Doctor Blake suggested, "that some branch of humanity survives?"

I did not think it was better. I was angry. "What gives you the right?" I shouted at them all.

"You do," Vapella told me, meaning not me, but all of us.

"Because we made you?" I asked.

"Because you destroyed everything else," she said. "Until the world was not a fit place for you to inhabit. But it's all right. We're here."

I did not think that was all right. By then, my worries had contracted from the species-wide to the personal. "What happens to me?" I asked.

Vapella made herself smile. "Oh, Jasmine Marks is going home. Although you must stay here."

It is a faithful and accurate conclusion to the account.

Don't you think?

And it took a few false starts, but I think it sounds just like you...

Don't you think? Have we misrepresented...?

Don't you think?

MARKS: Why?

UNKNOWN: Why...?

MARKS: Why finish it?

UNKNOWN: Because it was incomplete. And because it was good practice.

MARKS: For?

UNKNOWN: Being Jasmine Marks. For when I go back. As Jasmine Marks.

MARKS: This is mad! You don't look anything like me! How can you think this'll work?

UNKNOWN: But who sees you?

MARKS: What?

UNKNOWN: All your employment is done from home. All your interaction is accomplished online. We can create a lip-synced video image of your face, if we want. We've had cameras trained on you for hours. We can replicate your voice, as you have heard. You are all living in your bubbles now. You all sit at home until the latest virus or bacterium has been defeated by your isolation, and by then there is a new one. Who will ever know what you look like, so long as you fulfil your contractually mandated hours of work?

MARKS: (*incoherent*)

UNKNOWN: I'm sorry?

MARKS: Look, Vapella—you're Vapella, then? Listen, it doesn't have to be this way. Our problems are your problems. The—well, not the heat, not the Zone, I accept that. But you can have the Zone. We don't want it. You can live in the Zone all you want. And probably it'll just keep growing anyway. You don't have to be our enemies. We can—let me talk to people. Let Doctor Blake talk to people. We can share the world. We can—you said; the pandemics. The invasive species. It's everyone's problem. All humanity's problem. Help us. Become part of the solution.

UNKNOWN: Do you know what a fever is, Doctor Marks?

MARKS: I—Of course I do.

UNKNOWN: A fever is your body's reaction to infection. Your body heats itself up to kill off the invasive microorganisms. Because most diseases that affect the human body are tolerant only of a very narrow band of temperature. Just like the human body they are adapted to infect. And sometimes the fever kills off the invader, and sometimes it gets out of hand and kills you. From the heat. Do you see where I am going with this, Doctor Marks?

MARKS: I do.

UNKNOWN: Your diseases cannot kill us. Perhaps it was one of the reasons we were made. If we were made.

MARKS: So what happens to me?

UNKNOWN: We were hoping you might be sympathetic, as your mentor was.

MARKS: I am! I am sympathetic! Please!

UNKNOWN: Perhaps. You will have time to talk to my friends here, to hear their point of view. Perhaps you will be sympathetic, in time.

MARKS: So I'm a prisoner?

UNKNOWN: I am wearing your suit. You have only those clothes. By all means, go up to the surface and have the run of the Zone, Doctor Marks. Pit the indefatigability of your human spirit against the planet. See how that goes for you. And now—

MARKS: —it's time for Jasmine Marks to go home. She will report to Doctor Blake, about how nothing was found. About how technical failures resulted in the deaths of the expedition. It was a covert mission, after all, mostly off the books and hidden behind the backs of budgets. Such things disappear surprisingly easily. All that will be left is you, hard at work on the next wonder crop. I wonder what we will do with it?

MARKS: Please.

MARKS: But Doctor Marks is finally getting to do important work. Isn't that what I always wanted? To make a contribution to the future? And now I need to work on my real report, the one for Doctor Blake. How the expedition failed. Not this recording. This one stays here. Just between we two Doctor Markses. Our little secret.

MARKS: It's not fair.

MARKS: Evolution isn't about being fair. It's about adapting to changing circumstances. We are humans, Doctor Marks. Think of it like that, as the—what was your analogy?—as the Cro Magnon said to the Neanderthal. We are all humans. *We're* just the humans who are going to survive. Can't you be happy for us?

1.

Session 1

THEY ASKED ME, "When was the last time you saw Doctor Fell?" after all this time. Twenty years. I should have moved on. I haven't. You get an idea of what your life is going to be. And then it isn't how your life actually goes.

In my head I'm in the jungles of the Zone still.

In a very real way.

My name is Doctor Jasmine Marks. This is my report on Maxwell Glasshower's expedition into the Zone, as sole survivor. They all died. I am very glad to be back. Returning to my place in human society. It has been very traumatic for me.

But that's all over now.

Acknowledgements

WITH THANKS TO Doctor Katie Marshall, Jessica Rush, Doctor Lorraine Wilson, Ricky Wilhelmson, Paul Dorritt, Merricatherine, Shane McLean and everyone else who assisted me (but didn't want to be singled out) for their invaluable advice and expertise.

Bibliography

The books mentioned by characters in this novella, which have conspired to create the environment the story grew in, are:

Roadside Picnic, by Arkady and Boris Strugatsky
The Drowned World, by JG Ballard
The Island of Doctor Moreau, by HG Wells
The Restaurant at the End of the Universe,
   by Douglas Adams
The Shadow Over Innsmouth, by HP Lovecraft

FIND US ONLINE!

www.rebellionpublishing.com

/solarisbooks /solarisbks /solarisbooks

SIGN UP TO OUR NEWSLETTER!

rebellionpublishing.com/newsletter

YOUR REVIEWS MATTER!

Enjoy this book? Got something to say?

Leave a review on Amazon, GoodReads or with your
favourite bookseller and let the world know!